a light on the runway

*For Terry and Carroll —
Every life needs
some adventure !
Janet Haack*

Enjoy !

Cover Design by Todd Haack

A Light on the Runway

An autobiography:
Janet Haack

First Printing

ISBN# 1-933678-14-3

Library of Congress Control Number: 2006931499

A Palmland Publishing Product

Palmland
Publishing
Pine Island, Florida

Introduction for A LIGHT ON THE RUNWAY

Years ago, I was editing an unpolished, but thoroughly readable, manuscript from a local diamond dealer. When an especially unique passage came up, I would call my wife, Miriam, in to look at it. After the third one of these "calls," Miriam's comment was, "I wonder what his wife was doing while he was flying over the jungles of South America?" And I wondered the same thing.

When Don Haack's successful biographical account (*Bush Pilot in Diamond Country*) of his early diamond "mining" days in the rivers of Brazil and British Guiana was published, his readers also asked, "What's his wife doing during all these adventures?" We sure knew she wasn't eating *bon- bons* and watching the "soaps." Not when the nearest neighbors were Macusi Indians and town was a six day trek through the jungle to the closest airstrip, Georgetown, being 2 ½ hours from there by air. *A Light on the Runway*, by Jan Haack, answers the question.

When Jan wasn't living the adventures with her husband, she was doing "everyday" things like having a baby in a Catholic hospital on the coast, prodding boa constrictors to leave the bathroom, confronting the occasional drifter while holding a small child on one hip and wearing a pistol on the other, and washing clothes on rocks at the river…you know, average stuff every housewife does.

To be honest, it took some urging from me and others to convince Jan her story and that of her young family's was not only quite different, but a very personal recounting that displayed a quiet courage and an amazing love for and confidence in her husband.

Those of you who know Jan are aware of her charming, elegant demeanor. After reading her book, your comment will be, "Wow, I had no idea…!"

Robert Fulton, Jr. Ph.D.
Editor-in-Chief
Palmland Publishing

About author Janet Haack

Born in Washington, D.C., Janet Adrienne Mills grew up in Birmingham, Michigan studying classical dance there and in Detroit, New York and Chicago. In 1950, she left for the University of Wisconsin in Madison. A journalism major specializing in women's issues, Jan met her future husband, Don Haack, in her freshman year.

Just over a year after their marriage, Jan and Don left for the interior of British Guiana and began the adventure, which this book and her husband's *Bush Pilot in Diamond Country* cover.

After returning to the United States Jan continued to help her husband with his various enterprises, one of which led the two of them and their four children to live on the island of Grenada for fourteen years. While there Jan produced The Grenada Visitor's Guide, a monthly publication for tourists and helped Don run the Rum Runner, a popular excursion for cruise ship passengers visiting the island.

Now living on 70 acres north of Charlotte, North Carolina, Jan and Don own and operate Donald Haack Diamonds and Fine Gems, neatly closing the circle of interest in diamonds from mines to customer. As an advocate of the arts, Jan is on the Board of Directors of Opera Carolina.

For Don
my beloved companion through
this journey called life

My great thanks…

to Editor, Dr. Robert Fulton whose ever-present sense of humor made me laugh while revising…

to Don for his patience and guidance through all things electronic…

to our son, Todd, for a beautiful cover design…

to our wonderful family and friends for their suggestions and encouragement

Table of Contents

a light on the runway

An autobiography by
Janet Haack

edited by
Robert W. Fulton

Prologue

A cold April rain spattered against the dark windows of the air terminal, blurring the runway lights beyond. Northwest had delayed announcing the arrival of Don's flight until my stomach completed a square knot. I'd paced the rows between waiting passengers for an eternity already, wanting to get our reunion behind us. Then suddenly I spotted Don running for cover.

"Hi, Hon," he grinned, grabbing me in a familiar bear hug. He had been gone three months. A lifetime. One third of our married lifetime.

His grin turned sheepish, uncertain. "Brought you something," he said, reaching deep into his tweed coat pocket. *A diamond? An emerald? Some other exotic South American souvenir?* He'd meant to be gone on this exploratory trip for three weeks. Those turned into months, with little communication between us. After two months I wrote him a letter I'm glad I never sent. Of course I couldn't send it. I didn't know where he was! In this era I'd have rung his cell phone or dialed up the GPS connection. But this was 1955 and such advanced technology was years away.

"Her name is Chibi," he offered, as he tenderly placed a shivering ball of striped fur in my outstretched hands. "The Brazilians use that word for 'little diamond.'"

My life with Don began four years earlier at the University of Wisconsin. Or perhaps with our wedding last July. Looking back, I realize it began with the gift of this tiny member of the ocelot family. Our lives would not resemble our friends' lives. The years would hold not only the unusual, but the uncertain. We would have no game plan to follow. Instead, we'd take our cue from Don's prophetic phrase I'd heard often from our first date onwards: "We've only one life to live—so let's live it!"

As we sloshed through the last ice puddle to our car, Chibi tucked safely inside my coat, Don explained how his native guides shot her mother in the Brazilian bush a couple of weeks before. "Then we found her, just a day or two old, and I've been feeding her formula with an eye-dropper every two hours since," he boasted.

"Do you think she can survive? It's so cold here, and she's so tiny." Now Chibi was warm and comfortable, but *I* was shivering. I settled into the passenger seat and looked down at my 'gift.' Two very round dark eyes peered out from under my coat and my heart melted.

Don started the car and sat back against the driver's seat. Turning to me with a look that meant, "pay attention," he said confidently, "She'll survive, Jan. She's a plucky little cat and she's made it this far with only me for a mother. She'll make it until *we* take her back to South America."

1

Preparing for Adventure

The details of the expedition spilled out as we headed home from Milwaukee's Billy Mitchell Field. "There are diamonds in the border river between British Guiana and Brazil. We'll set up the dredging equipment 250 miles inland from the coast, build our house there, and. . . oh yeah, we're going to have to buy a plane and learn how to fly. Most of the rivers are barely navigable and the Indians walk everywhere they need to go."

Two hundred and fifty miles from civilization? Learning to fly a plane? Setting up a diamond mining company and leaving our jobs, home, and families in four months? After three months alone, sometimes worried, sometimes fuming, it was hard for me to take it all in.

"It sounds so exotic!" gushed one of my fellow employees at the county agent's office in Milwaukee, where I'd been hired on graduation from the University of Wisconsin to create a department of consumer information.

"What an experience! How I wish I were you!" others chimed in, eyes wide open with wonder. "Aren't you excited?"

It was hard to tell what I was, given the frantic pace of those four months. It's difficult to remember what drove me. Don's unending enthusiasm? I agreed with friends that I was "the last person in the world to move to the jungle." I grew up in Birmingham, Michigan, studied classical ballet there, in Detroit, New York and Chicago, but ballet required a commitment I wasn't prepared to give when my dad suggested a career in women's journalism . My roommate in Ann Emery Hall introduced me to her cousin, Don. I have only myself to blame, or take credit, for our life, since it was *I* who asked *him* for our first date—a walk across the campus on a gorgeous October day, too beautiful for studying. An epic walk, that.

The two of us hardly had time to think during those hectic weeks of preparation for a move to South America. We'd dash to the airfield after work. He'd leave his brother's diamond store an hour before I left my desk so that he could finish his hour's flight lesson. Then I'd go up for an hour before dusk and we'd write it all down in our log books before heading home for "dinner," which in those days and at those late hours was usually a chocolate banana milkshake with an egg in it. Many were nights when I had a talk to give to a women's group, so Don's logbook filled up faster than mine.

Don had speeches to give, too, on the expedition he'd just concluded. Family, friends and new admirers were wide-eyed and of course Chibi was a main attraction. In my job, I had weekly appearances on television and radio, enlightening housewives as to the best buys of the week in their grocery stores. Chibi went along, even though she had nothing whatsoever to do with food-buying recommendations. Who cared about the availability of asparagus when there was this sweet and beautiful little tiger cat?

Don and I squeezed in a break to drive to Cape Cod for a vacation in July. My mother loaned us her red and

Feeding Chibi.

white convertible to make the trip even more fun, and Chibi graced the back of the driver's seat as if she'd been born there. On the Cape she learned to swim in salt water. It was that or be left pacing the shore while Don and I enjoyed our swim. Her attachment to us was as profound as ours to her. At night we would put her to bed on the floor of our closet, but in the morning discover her nestled between our heads. She would awaken one of us with her cold nose in the ear.

As the first of September rolled around, our lists of things to do grew longer. Don was meeting with prospective investors and manufacturers of diving and dredging equipment. That left me to search out items as varied as chemical toilets and a year's supply of "Love That Red" lipstick. Two trunks that Chibi and I used for games of hide-and-seek stood in the middle of our apartment living room. Trunk number one contained everything from dishtowels to a .22 caliber rifle, two portable typewriters, Merck's Medical Manual, and a Scrabble game. Mundane articles filled trunk two: clothes, shoes, books on learning to speak Portuguese, our pistols, and several cans of Saniflush. *Does one need Saniflush in the jungle?*

Our wedding presents went into storage. I gave away houseplants. I got a perm. We secured certificates of sanity from the health department. Don said I needed leather gloves. Got them. *No time for questions, just do it.* We got our tetanus, typhoid, smallpox, yellow fever, and cholera shots. Then my physical required for a pilot's license turned up something unexpected. I was pregnant. *Timing is everything.*

"Come here a sec, Hon," Don called from the living room. "I got my maps of South America and thought you might like to see where we're going." I followed his finger on the map spread out on top of Trunk One. It traced the curve of the West Indies and jumped the short distance from Trinidad to a tiny country on the northernmost coast of South America.

"Here it is, Georgetown, the only real city. We'll build our house about 250 miles in from the coast...about here." His finger stopped at a sharp bend in the border river between Brazil and British Guiana, which we were now calling "B.G." as locals there did.

We made reservations on Pan American leaving New Orleans for South America on September 16, 1955. We'd purchased a Piper Super Cub, a two seater. Since it was green and so small, we dubbed it "Grasshopper" and both of us delighted in flying it. Don qualified for his pilot's license with 40 hours, but I was short by an hour or two when our departure time arrived. The two of us would fly the Grasshopper from Milwaukee to New Orleans where it would be boxed and crated for shipment by freighter to British Guiana. It would be Don's first long cross-country. We both looked forward to a last little bit of relaxation then on a commercial airline with someone else in charge of the flight deck.

Now that everyone knew I was expecting a baby, awe turned to disbelief. Or disapproval in my parents' case: "Let Don go and you stay here where there are doctors to be trusted, and hospitals, and...." From the outset Mother and Dad had not been pleased with the idea of our living in a "foreign country."

But our course was set, the last load of laundry done— for the fifth time— the new apartment tenants actually started to move in, the plane was packed, and what's so difficult about having a baby? I'd have chained up our own daughters had they presented us with this scenario. There is a fine line, often blurred, between courage and stupidity. There was nothing to do but take off!

2

And We're Off!

At chilly dawn on the fifteenth of September, we hugged the Milwaukee "bon voyage" contingent and climbed in behind our single engine. The pressures of the last few days were evident.

"I don't know what in hell you're going to do with a hat in the jungle," he grumbled as I shoved the hatbox once again behind my head

"Well, it's not bothering you up there in front so just forget about my hat. I need to look decent when we arrive in Georgetown, don't I?" I countered. Who knows why I felt I needed a hat, though in the 1950's young ladies wore hats with style and were not "dressed" without one. Perhaps I was trying to preserve my image, or was taking along evidence of civilization, or a symbol of gracious living. I needed my little white hat, that's all. But I never did get that box properly stowed and the damned thing fell forward on my head every thirty seconds for the next twelve hours.

Don had forty hours under his belt that morning and a brand new pilot's license in his pocket. He also had a ferocious headwind predicted for the entire trip down to Louisiana with only ten hours of daylight left at that time of year. The first few hours we flew a couple hundred feet off the ground where the headwinds were not as strong. A few quick stops for gas allowed us to take our weary bottoms out of their leather prisons and wake up our legs, but as dark fell, we were still far from New Orleans.

The night-time approach and landing in New Orleans were epic. Don described them vividly in his book, *Bush Pilot in Diamond Country.* My description might vary a little. Since I wasn't actively engaged in the flying, I had more time to devote to sheer terror.

Don yelled into the back seat "We'll miss our connections if we wait 'til morning. It's a clear night. What say we keep going?"

I had a choice? The next thought came unbidden: this would be Don's first stab at night flying.

At long last the rows of tiny red runway lights came in sight and Don made contact with the tower operators. But their instructions still left us puzzled. "It sure does look like a water runway down there," Don called back to me. Then, just as he should have cut the power to settle down, he gave it full throttle instead and pulled sharply into the air. "Dammit! What do they think I've got on this thing… pontoons?"

"What's the matter, 94 Bravo? Your approach looked perfect." The words came as we flew over the runway, concrete stretched solidly beneath us from its beginning right at the water's edge.

"Sorry, New Orleans. This is 94 Bravo. We'll go around again and come in this time, for good"

My legs shook as I climbed out from the back seat and hopped to the ground. Don hurried over to a man standing at the fence and motioned for me to follow.

"This is Mr. Fisher, Jan, our shipping agent for the Grasshopper. He's been waiting all afternoon and evening and had just about given up on us."

"I knew you'd have to be in tonight," Mr. Fisher was saying, "if you're going to make your PanAm flight in the morning. Welcome to New Orleans. I'll see to the plane and then treat you to a night out in our great city!"

I dashed off to find the nearest phone booth to call my parents and let them know we'd made it safely and, as I lied, uneventfully. It was nearly 11:00 p.m. in Michigan, but I knew worry would keep them awake.

"We're fine and looking forward to a good night's sleep," I reassured them. "What? Oh, yes, I'm feeling great and we'll be off on our adventure in the morning. Take care and I'll write every chance I get. Bye!"

At the hotel, we tossed our bags on the bed and quickly unpacked what we hoped would serve at appropriate "night on the town" garb.

"I'd rather be putting on my p.j's," I said wistfully to Don as I slipped into heels and hose. "But Mr. Fisher is so nice to want to show us the nightlife. I guess we can sleep on the plane tomorrow."

The good night's sleep we both wanted so badly turned out to be a couple of hours' worth, fully dressed, and lying on top of the hotel's bedspread. We'd done Brennan's and The Olde Absinthe house with Mr. Fisher and in spite of my delicate condition, it was after three in the morning when we stumbled back to the hotel. We had to get up at 5:00 a.m.

It was still dark as we sleepily climbed into the hotel limousine, I with my hat properly on my head.

"With only two hours' sleep it's a good thing we're relying on someone else to fly us southward," Don observed.

First stop was Merida, Mexico where half a dozen little boys chattering in Spanish followed us around, as if we were the Pied Piper. They wanted to "shine" my white shoes.

Janet Haack

Later, in Managua, Nicaragua, engine trouble left us with the prospect of "an indefinite stay." Airline transport took us to a small hotel where Don and I quickly found a bed secretly hoping it would take hours, maybe days, to put the plane back together again. But we had no such luck. Roused from our sleep by a sharp knock on the door, we found a taxi waiting for us outside. Next stop Panama City!

"Well, *now* things are beginning to look up!" I said happily as our taxi pulled up to a beautiful hotel set amidst the palms. A lovely room with a bed that promised a full night's sleep, a vine-covered terrace overlooking the swimming pool now lent a decidedly positive side to our journey. Dressed for dinner, we eagerly advanced on the dining room, intent on making the most of our paid-for-by-the-airline stopover. But as Don tucked merrily into his food, I was not quite ready to eat for two and struggled to enjoy a chicken sandwich and glass of gingerale. This adventure thing was not, so far, all it was cracked up to be. It was to get worse.

The mountainous island of Trinidad offered us the Queen's Park Hotel, in the heart of Port of Spain. Gorgeous island, gorgeous hotel, but mostly we took turns occupying the gorgeous bathroom for three days of intestinal rampage.

The night before we were to take off for our final destination, Georgetown, British Guiana, we suddenly felt better and walked down to dinner on the terrace surrounded with swaying palms and fragrant frangipanis. After eating we felt revived and hired a driver, Ishmael, to drive us through the warm tropical night to hear our first steel band music. The melodies the dark skinned boys coaxed from their ungainly instruments enchanted me: soft sounds floating on a soft breeze—yes, this is more like what I'd envisioned.

Next morning Ishmael was waiting for us in the hotel lobby.

"I take you and the "nice missus" for a short drive outside Port of Spain so you see some of our island," he invited. "It only cost five dollah."

Don felt compelled to barter since it was Ishmael's idea, not ours. So our "tree dolluh" tour took us through the lush green mountains rising a short distance from the turquoise waters of the sea, as they do on most of the Caribbean Islands. The low white buildings of the Imperial College stood out against that rich green background. And later the dark skin of an African woman and her daughter stood out against the brilliant white cascade of a waterfall at Blue Basin, as the two swayed and chanted, hip-deep in the water, three lighted candles floating in front of them. This encounter, so foreign to me and so personal yet tranquil, erased the frenzied feeling that had been my sole companion for the preceding weeks. My fatigue vanished with that Blue Basin visit, and we were truly on our way to the adventure so long planned. Thank you, Ishmael.

3

Capital City

It was late afternoon when we stepped off the ramp onto Atkinson Field, a network of concrete runways creating a curious bare spot in the midst of the surrounding tangle of jungle. Built as an airbase by the Americans during WWII, it connected to the capital city of Georgetown, British Guiana by what was laughingly referred to as a road.

"This is the longest road in B.G.—both literally and figuratively,"Don chuckled as our taxi headed toward Georgetown.

At amazing speed we careened around most of the potholes, narrowly avoiding scrawny chickens, mangy dogs, rickety bicycles pedaled by unskilled riders bearing semi-terrified passengers, and naked toddlers towed by determined women under heavy baskets. Our black driver leaned on the horn most of the way "playing chicken" with oncoming vehicles—not all of them cars. As we approached the city outskirts heavy wooden carts pulled by bullocks joined the melee.

As we pulled up in front of a tall white wooden building in the center of the city, I was grateful to be alive and with our baby intact.

"The Tower Hotel," Don announced. "Let's hope they

have a room available for a week or two. Our 'Grasshopper' and the trunks should arrive by then."

But our $30 per night rate would not be reduced even when we guaranteed them a month's stay. Back in the taxi we calculated our living expenses. "We'll stay the night and then move somewhere else," Don said decisively. "This hotel obviously won't fit in our budget."

The next day we moved to the Woodbine Hotel a few blocks down the main street and around the corner. It would become our home away from home when we came back into Georgetown from the interior. The proprietor, Mac Wiltshire, an amiable brown fellow with wavy gray hair, greeted us with a broad smile. He booked us in, showed us to our room up the stairs, and announced dinner would be served at seven o'clock.

The little room was adequate: twin iron beds with mosquito netting knotted above each sat against either wall, the space between them leading to a veranda which overlooked the street. Fortunately there was a door to shut out the clatter of donkey carts and the ever-present blare of car horns. The room would do for a couple of weeks.

It was clean, had a shower and sink, and it fit in the budget. We were in good spirits as we unpacked and cleaned up for dinner.

"Not a bad meal," I commented on the way back upstairs. "They do eat a lot of rice here, don't they? But at least the soup wasn't greasy. I can't say I care for the ice cream much. What in the world do they make it wi…E-e-e-k!" The ugly little lizard scurried across the wall above the doorway.

"Oh, come now," Don chided, pulling me into our room. "It's just a little lizard, and you'll see them everywhere down here. They eat insects so you should be grateful for them."

Had I grown up in Florida, no doubt I'd be used to "creatures." But as a young lady from suburban Detroit, I equated lizards with mice, neither of which should occupy our living quarters. It would take a while before I stopped jumping at the sight of lizards and I did grow to appreciate their appetite for insects. But when I discovered two more out on the veranda that night, I made up my mind to check out return flights to the 'States as soon as possible. Culture shock was setting in.

Bright sunshine next morning lightened my outlook on life, so I decided to postpone my trip Stateside at least until after breakfast.

Two newspaper reporters bounded up the front steps of the Woodbine and nearly pounced on us at our table for an interview. It didn't matter what we told them. They had already concluded we were in British Guiana to seek a fortune and that's the way it came out in the next day's paper.

"They can't even get our name spelled correctly," I groaned as I read the article to Don as he ate breakfast the following morning. "Thank heaven we're old news today and that's over." We should've been so fortunate.

After that article was printed, we became the target of those we would dub "the diamond bums." They came in all ages and stages of sobriety; their proposals were the same. Each knew exactly where "El Dorado" lay. Each urged that with our money and his know-how, we could all end up with a fortune.

Don discouraged all politely and firmly, though one sad, sad pair of young Americans brought out the "Dutch uncle" in him. We listened to their tale of woe. Having deprived their families of dinners out, movies, all small luxuries for over a year, while they devoured books on South America, they had saved $700, a fortune to them. They had even eaten grasshoppers because that is what one book had suggested would be necessary to survive.

They had bought cases of flares and canned heat, hoping to sell them to the natives. None of their hopes had materialized. Don was as understandingly kind as he knew how.

"This will not be what you want to hear," he advised. "But it is a lesson well learned while you're young. Don was a wise old twenty-four at this time. Take as many photos as you can with your movie camera and try to get a story together with them. You might be able to book some speaking engagements back home. Now use your round trip ticket to get back to your families. It has been an adventure. That's all. Someday you'll laugh about it when you tell your grandchildren." We never saw them again.

Gasconne was more of a problem. Showing up drunk one lunchtime, he, too, knew the way to El Dorado. Day after day, he'd corner us at our lunch table. He always smelled of alcohol and his greasy black hair did not endear him to us further. Ushered out time after time, he sent henchmen to vouch for his Midas methods. This was getting to be a pain until Don's "no" became "NO!" Gasconne and his thugs may have faded into the distance but I always felt they were lurking behind the palm trees somewhere.

Morning after sunny morning, Don and I set out walking the few blocks into the center of Georgetown. A wide straight gravel path, bordered by huge Flamboyant trees providing much-needed shade, stretched between the two canals that separated the main boulevard. Georgetown, constructed four feet below sea level, kept her nose above water by a seawall holding out the Caribbean. We spent those first days in the city checking out stores, government offices, banks, and distributors of anything edible or mechanical we might need in the interior.

Soon after our arrival, we sought out the police station to obtain our gun permits. We knew it wouldn't be easy, given the small arsenal packed in our trunks: our .22 caliber semi-automatic pistols, Remington twelve-gauge pump shotgun, a Winchester lever-action 30/30 rifle and over a thousand rounds of ammunition.

The poker-faced officer in charge of permits needed to be convinced that each gun was absolutely necessary. Don did a good job of overcoming the bureaucrat's reluctance to issue the permits, without a bribe. Then we got to the issue of my pistol.

"No!" he shouted, patience tried. "I see no reason for a female to have such a weapon, and I doubt that Mistress Haack can even shoot it accurately. That makes for a very dangerous situation." He sat back, pleased with this argument.

"Well, sir," Don said, "I guess I have to admit now that my wife is a better shot than I am. She would gladly give you a demonstration."

The officer declined this exhibition, but clearly did not like such an extraordinary request. We discussed this for over an hour. Keeping his cool, Don summed up the risks of leaving a defenseless wife alone in the bush without protection. I looked as helpless, yet skilled, as possible and as lunchtime approached we won our case. Permit number four was issued.

At last our long list of tasks dwindled to nothing, but still our trunks had not arrived. Nor had our "Grasshopper." We'd rounded up an agent to clear everything through customs. We walked the city from one side to the next, acquainting ourselves with the Staebroek Market and all its sounds and smells. We discovered *The Brown Betty* where that odd ice cream made from evaporated milk was sold. We visited Booker's Department Store where I learned a new language—*English* English—and the Bank of Nova Scotia.

We visited St. George's Cathedral, at that time the tallest all-wooden structure in the world. One Sunday we were invited to a new acquaintance's house after church, where we discovered the local Sunday afternoon ritual is to get drunk. The following Sunday, thinking there must be some better pastime, we went home, ate lunch, read the paper, took a walk along the seawall, came back to the hotel and —nothing to do.

"I know," Don offered brightly. "How about a game of strip poker?" Okay, so we were desperate

"Sorry, no cards."

"No problem," he offered, taking out the cardboard from his newly laundered shirt. "We'll make some."

Clearly having nothing to do is far worse than having too much to do. It was a thoroughly engrossing afternoon and evening and we did laugh a lot.

Hurricane Janet delayed our trunks which were now captive on a mercy mission to the hard-hit island of Grenada. So our plane arrived first, complete with a huge hole in the crate and matching hole in the wing. Don went on the warpath.

"It will take weeks to repair the wing and we're already well into October," he ranted. "Christmas rains begin in early December and I'd hoped to be building barges for the mining equipment and hiring workers by this time."

Now it looked like we'd barely get the mining operation started before the rains came, the rivers rose and it became dangerous to work in raging waters. To add to this frustration, Her Majesty's Customs weren't as bent on releasing the plane from bond as we were. The delay was getting to our nerves.

"I'm taking that plane out tomorrow," Don whispered to me in the privacy of our hotel room. "I'm going to sneak it out."

"A 1,000 pound plane?" My doubt only challenged him further.

"This is British Guiana, remember?" he offered mysteriously, "Wait and see. I'll have her out tomorrow."

The removal of the plane from Her Majesty's Customs warehouse is vividly described in Don's book, *Bush Pilot in Diamond Country*. By the following afternoon, a customs warehouse had been lifted from its base by a ship's crane, the crate housing our Grasshopper had been freed and loaded aboard a truck and was on its way to Atkinson Field, Don sitting beside the driver, whistling and looking very pleased with himself.

"It's gone, Mr. Haack, sir! It's **gone**!" panted our customs agent next morning. He was truly in a state of discomfort as he mopped his brow.

"It's all right, Morris, Don said quietly. "Everything is okay. I'll worry about our plane. Just forget about it and find out when our trunks are scheduled to get in. Call us then."

Fortunately, Don discovered he could repair the wing at Atkinson instead of sending to the 'States for a new one. For two weeks John Rix, a local aviation engineer with an American A&E license — required in order to be approved by local officials—worked doggedly on the wing with Don. Most of those trips over the Atkinson "road" I avoided, though once in a while I'd tag along, being useful fetching tools and cutting fabric patches. I also needed to measure the plane for a massive form-fitting tarpaulin, which I was sewing-by hand. It would take a while to build a hangar near our house in the interior and without protection against the tropical sun, the exterior of the plane would have a short life. It needed a wrap.

I made a new friend, Marie Lyder, the wife of my obstetrician in Georgetown. She, too, was expecting a baby and we hit it off right away with that much in common. In turn, Marie introduced me to Pamela Wheating, wife of Tom Wheating, head of one of the largest firms in Georgetown, Wheating & Richter. Pam was mistress *extraordinaire* of an imposing white home next to Mercy Hospital. Both faced the Parade Ground, a large open grassy square where military exercises were conducted.

The three of us would have tea together. Marie and Pam, both being "take charge" kind of women would guide my uneducated footsteps to the proper shops for a layette. Pam drove me to the Staebrook Market one day for a basket big enough for a newborn, and then to shops for soft blue fabric – Don and I were sure we'd have a boy—quilting, lace edging, and a seamstress to put it all together.

My new role as "purchasing agent" for Haack Mining Company was alternately fun and frustrating. Shillings and pence gave me fits and I needed a pencil and paper to equate American value by doing a seven-times-twenty-four-move-back-two-decimal-points routine when presented with a seven-shilling item. I tried the idiot system of paying in dollars— four shillings per dollar I could grasp— and just wait for the change. Then I'd go to the bank and get more dollars. Seemed a good plan to me, but when I described it Marie and Pam gasped for breath between fits of laughter.

"Our baby's not going to wear diapers," I told Don one evening as he showered off the grease and dust of his day. "He's going to wear 'nappies.' That's what they call them-nappies." He didn't seem very engaged in this conversation covering my shopping difficulties.

"I might as well get used to the fact that I'll never get exactly what I want," I continued petulantly. "I had to spend hours today describing an undershirt to the store clerk," I exaggerated.

"An undershirt? Why?" Clearly he was more concerned

with things like getting our airplane to fly and the mining operation started, and was only paying half attention.

"Because they are not undershirts! They're vests! Who ever heard of such a thing. A vest is part of a man's three-piece suit for pity's sake. Besides, whenever I do finally learn the correct word, Booker's is out of it and they and every other store in town are always expecting a shipment of them in a few months."

"Well, our little tyke isn't due for several months, so you'll have time to figure it all out," he offered, far too sensibly for my state of frustration. "And by the way, I've found out where we can get the milk you're supposed to be drinking. Harry's wife's uncle or some such, works for the government and he's promised to get some milk to her regularly. All we have to do is supply the bottles."

I had yet to discover powdered milk and this was good news. And so it was that my two empty rum bottles found their way across the city from the Woodbine every morning by bicycle messenger and back again in the afternoon. Warm and lumpy, the milk was not appealing, but everyone had gone to such effort to supply it that I was grateful, as I held my breath and drank it down. I began to long for our own house in the interior of British Guiana and our own cows.

As repairs to the "Grasshopper's" wing neared completion, we made plans for our move, now a week away, 250 miles into the interior. Don was taking a rare day off from his work at Atkinson and we were at lunch in the Woodbine when he suddenly shoved his chair back and jumped up, hand outstretched, broad smile on his face, saying "Caesar! This is great surprise. Come meet Jan."

I turned to meet the man I'd heard so much about, the one who'd befriended Don and his brother Bob on their first trip to South America earlier in the year. Caesar was the one who had offered to bed and board Don and me at his ranch until we got our own home built at the mine site. The tanned and good-looking Caesar shook my hand warmly as he sized me up and down., no doubt calculating how long I'd last back in the bush.

" Yan," he said, with his charming Russian accent, "I am so glad to meet you at last. Don told Nellie and me many good things about you" he continued, referring to his wife. "He did not tell us you were this attractive."

Smooth,. Fortunately I could blush on command.

"I came into town for the races this weekend. I hope the two of you will join me on Saturday to see "The Russell" run," he said, referring to his newly acquired racehorse.

This sounded like a lot a fun for two people who had little diversion from the responsibility of getting a new business going. As Don brought Caesar up to date with our various frustrations and accomplishments, I envisioned a day at the Turf Club.

And what a day it was. Don and I were both new to the sport of kings and immediately took a fancy to the pageantry, the gorgeous horses, the excitement, and the 'tea' that was served at afternoon break. Crab shells stuffed with delicious crabmeat; tiny cucumber, tomato, or cheese sandwiches; dainty sweets; and plenty of strong English tea. What fun! All the more because Caesar and I were winning our bets. Luck, of course, on my part, more skill on Caesar's. It wasn't long before I realized that gambling gave him a fair portion of his entertainment in life.

The following Monday we booked passage on BG Airways' Friday flight to Good Hope for Harry, our new foreman, and me. Caesar would fly inland with Don in our Grasshopper, showing him the checkpoints along the route to Good Hope, Caesar and Nellie's ranch on the northern edge of the Rupununi savannah, alongside the Ireng River. The DC-3 flew on to Lethem from Good Hope on alternate

Fridays. Lethem was a small village at the southern end of the savannah. These were mail and cargo runs and passengers were incidental. We'd sit in the metal bucket seats lined up on either side of the belly of the plane.

The next few days brought plenty of emotions. For Don it was relief at the end to plane and customs problems, elation at the prospect of *getting started*. For me there was more than a bit of trepidation. I'd be leaving two new and valued friends behind, as well as civilization. My sense of adventure fought with the feeling of safety and convenience in Georgetown: doctors, hospital, *Cable and Wireless* where we could be within telegraph reach of our families. Adventure won out.

Don and Caesar left early from Georgetown to get a head start and arrive at Good Hope when the DC-3 touched down. But one delay after another eventually put their takeoff to only a few minutes before Harry's and mine. Weighed in like cargo and marked down in pounds on the flight manifest , Harry and I sat and waited on flour sacks in a vast barn-like building called "The Ramp," the storage facility for everything being shipped to the interior from Georgetown. As the day wore on the morning sun beat down on our open metal shelter until I felt I was being roasted on a spit. It was so bizarre it was funny. Six weeks ago I'd been a young lady from suburbia. Today I was cargo.

After the passenger list was called out, Harry climbed the ladder ahead to give me a hand in. We were joined by a motley assortment of Indians and Brazilians, all of us nearly suffocating in the great metal plane when the doors closed and the pilots revved up the engines. "For better or for worse," I mused, as we climbed up and over a solid deep green floor of jungle.

In a deliciously cool hour and a half, I looked down and spotted the edge of open land called Rupununi Savannah.

I glanced at Harry. His dark eyes shone and a broad smile appeared under his dark moustache. He was home now. *And so, I guess, am I..*

4

Good Hope Ranch

As the DC-3 circled slowly over Good Hope airstrip, I twisted around in my bucket seat to peer out the small window behind me. I could easily make out a river winding through the flat, sand-colored ground below. A low white ranch house sprawled beside the river anchored and shaded by a few enormous trees. A jeep waited beside an airstrip a half a mile from the house. The landing was without incident, but my heart skipped several beats nonetheless. I'd heard so much about the Rupununi and now I was there, where we would make a home. The double doors of the plane opened and a hot wind blew into the cabin.

Harry helped me down the ladder and pointed out Nellie Gorinsky. Someone called to Harry and he dashed off, leaving me alone in the shade of the plane wing. I squinted back at the few staring onlookers and walked over to a tall, attractive dark-haired woman standing with two Indian girls.

"I'm Mrs. Haack, Mrs. Gorinsky," I offered.

"Who?"

"Mrs. Haack…Janet Haack…Don Haack's wife. He and—"

"Oh yes, oh yes," she interrupted, obviously annoyed. *But not by me.* I had read her thoughts. Caesar told us in Georgetown he'd be gone from home for a week. That stretched into three, and to Nellie, looking at the emptied plane, those three might become five.

"Caesar will be along with Don any time now, in our plane," I said cheerily. "They left Atkinson about the same time we did."

This information brought a smile to her face and turned her into the warm and welcoming woman I'd heard so much about. She put her arm around my shoulder, and we walked the dusty drive to the house together, as the others finished loading the jeep. It drove past us, the two Indian girls, squealing with delight, hung on to boxes and bags. Nellie and I talked, and my assurance grew that I'd found a new friend. I would be, for a time at least, living in the home of a wise and witty woman who could teach me much about living in "the bush." I wondered what she must think of me.

We reached the wide adobe house with its part grass, part corrugated aluminum roof, and ducked under the grape arbor shading the entrance. Since we were both thirsty after our walk in the noontime sun, Nellie took me immediately to the 'fridge' and showed me that it always stayed stocked with bottles of water, lemonade, and iced tea.

"Come. I'll show you where you and Don will sleep," she offered, setting off toward the opposite end of the house. "There's a frangipani tree right outside here," she said, reaching toward one of the front windows. She pushed the hinged pane out from the bottom and propped it open with a wooden slat. A heavenly fragrance filled the room. I looked out at the loveliest of white, waxen blooms with pale yellow throats. The blossoms were even more beautiful than their fragrance.

Nellie, now in the best of spirits, excused herself to start lunch. Caesar and Don would land at any minute. *This will be a special lunch.* I hoisted my suitcase onto the long straight arms of the Berbice chair by the window and slipped out of my dress into a pair of tan frontier pants and new pink shirt. *I think this is the way I'm supposed to look*

Nellie heard the faint buzz of our airplane engine before I did. Her ears, as mine would become, were tuned to sounds that meant a visitor by plane or jeep. She was on the front step ahead of me, and we stood under the arbor to watch the 'Grasshopper' settle onto the strip. As I looked at Nellie's face, I recognized her expression. She was so happy to see her husband again. I could imagine her feeling. Were Don and Caesar cut out of the same cloth? After all, Don had told me when he left for his first expedition that he'd be gone for three weeks. Then he was gone for the longest three months of my life.

Caesar and Don, no doubt drawn all the more quickly by the enticing smells of lunch, reached the house in no time. The four of us settled at one end of a long board table spread with dishes of roast beef, beans, farine, rice, bread, and some of the tomatoes recently unloaded from our plane. The conversation was lively, often punctuated by Nellie's low, rippling laughter. Weeks alone made her hungry for every snippet of news or gossip. Fed by the conversation as we were by the food, she was clearly delighted with our descriptions of minor successes and failures in Georgetown, and tales of my frustrations and challenges in a new environment.

Strong Brazilian coffee, laced with several spoons full of brown sugar and served in tiny doll-like cups, finished the meal.

"Except for breakfast," Nellie explained, "all our meals are like this, unless we're out of fresh beef. Sometimes we

Nellie, Jan and friend

get fresh lettuce or radishes from the garden, and once in a while my sister, Amy, brings us a piece of pork. She and her husband, Ben, raise a few pigs at Perara."

I paid close attention, gleaning bits of the Rupununi story and its characters. Don and I heard that three Gorinsky children, Pixie, Peter, and Luke, were not at home. The boys were at school, scheduled to be home for Christmas holidays and Pixie was off on a trip to the south savannah with her Aunt Amy.

The youngest, four-year-old Christopher, was off somewhere in the care of one of the Indian girls . . but would show up at any minute.

"Jan," Don shouted. "Don't scratch them!" he warned as I unconsciously raked my nails over my ankles below the table. "That's the bite of the cabourri fly I told you about. When it bites, it leaves a tiny blood spot under the skin. I know it itches, but scratching will only make it worse, so stop," he said and grabbed both my hands

"You'll get used to those, Yan," Caesar laughed, as I scrutinized the tiny red marks on my wrists and ankles.

"Have you?" I asked.

"No," he chuckled. "But I've only been here twenty-two years!"

The rest of that day and the next, I wasn't far from Don's side. I stepped gingerly around the outside of the house, wanting to be within calling distance for rescue, should I sight a poisonous snake or hungry leopard. Caesar called to us to watch the roundup of several of his cattle out on the savannah, and I watched from the jeep. But I still felt safer inside the house.

On Sunday afternoon, I was half sitting, half lying in one of the low sloping Berbice chairs lined up along the two long walls of the entrance gallery. There must be some trick to finding comfort in these, I thought. I shifted about on the long low-slung piece of furniture. *With a crescent cut out behind one's head, this would make an ideal shampoo chair.*

With the afternoon heat, the metal roof expanded and a small "pop-pop" punctuated the heavy silence. The hum of bees was suddenly drowned out by the roar of a jeep in front of the house. A young girl with dark hair and flashing eyes charged through the door.

"Mum? Oh, Mum? I'm home!" She stopped short when she noticed me, then breezed past with a surprised look that took in not only my making myself at home, but also my starched shirt, brand new frontier pants, and shiny new loafers. She found Nellie at the sewing machine in the back room. The two of them talked and laughed for a few minutes then came back to where I, the interloper, sat. Nellie introduced us and explained in a few words why Don and I were there.

"Come on you two," Nellie suggested. Let's go out to the kitchen and get some tea ready for Don and 'C.'"

We followed her through the sewing room and out the back door to a smaller building in the compound. As in rural America years ago, the kitchen because of the danger of fire, was detached from the main house. I saw that a big kettle sat on the back of the huge wood stove. It reminded me of my grandmother's house in Connecticut. I'd already made it clear to Nellie that I wanted to help in the kitchen, secretly hoping not to be taken up on the offer. This would be a good opportunity to show Pixie I was not just a pampered guest. I bravely offered to make muffins for tea. After all, here were two women who could regulate wood stove oven temperature. What could go wrong?

I've made better muffins. The five of us sat around the table having a wonderful catch-up on each other's recent escapades, so I hoped no one would really notice my culinary failure. We ate and sipped. Mariana, the Indian servant, sidled in and whispered in Pixie's ear. Pixie spluttered and nearly choked on her laughter.

"Sorry, Jan," she said, trying to keep a straight face. "But Mariana just asked me in her most serious tone what Miss Jan put in her muffins to make them so heavy."

"They're not my usual standard," I admitted, trying to be as good a sport about the joke as I could. "I have to get the hang of the ingredients and the stove. It's a sorry first attempt." Nellie looked sternly at Mariana who in turn looked sheepish. I smiled at her and winked. She'd asked a serious question, not meaning to hurt anyone's feelings. She ducked her head and scurried off to the kitchen.

Seventeen-year-old Pixie and I became friends and cohorts in that kitchen behind the house. She had been away at school in Georgetown since she was six, coming back to Good Hope on school holidays. This year was her first prolonged stay at home before heading to the University College of the West Indies in Jamaica, where she would study to become a doctor. So, she was almost as green as I in the ways of the wood stove, but far more adaptable to its peculiarities. Many times she patched up and disguised my poor efforts at culinary artistry. The two of us concocted desserts to the delight of all at the table, especially after a meal *sans* fresh beef and made up mostly of farine, rice and beans.

I watched Nellie make bread time after time and knew the day was near when I'd have to volunteer. The morning came when she accepted my offer and I bravely set out for the kitchen, *The Joy of Cooking* clutched purposefully in my hand.

"That's it, Jan," she said with encouragement, coming in to the kitchen as I began to knead the dough. "Now keep that up 'til it's smooth as a baby's bottom. Um-hum, you'll do all right."

And so I did. I forgot the salt a couple of times and never did perfect the oven temperature, but soon bread making became my order of the day.

Christmas was almost upon us. Pixie's two younger brothers, Peter, fourteen and Luke, nine arrived home from their school in Trinidad. The rest of us had all made trips to Georgetown to do our shopping, but Don and I had a hard time finding anything to send to our families in the States that was worth the postage. Until I discovered the Georgetown prison.

On a tip from my friend Marie, I took a taxi to the high-walled lock-up on the edge of town. In the tiny ante-room I asked about handiwork done by the inmates, and within minutes had a beautifully crafted wood inlay box in my hands. It was a perfect jewel box. The price was two dollars. There was no need to haggle.

Don and I scrounged through tiny handiwork shops, visited the Staebroek Market, searched down alleyways, and finally had a gift for each person at Good Hope. Our packages to our families flew off to the States with the contents and value plastered on the outside for customs purposes, and for each recipient to see before opening. I was actually glad to head back to the quiet and camaraderie of the Rupununi.

There, Nellie, Pixie, and I began the Christmas feast in earnest. Pixie and I concentrated on the cookie section of *Joy,* and Nellie worked on the fruitcakes. She had soaked the fruits in Demarara rum for weeks. The day before Christmas dawned gray and rainy, usual for the season they told us. Don and Pixie donned rain slickers and went off in search of a tree to decorate. We expected anywhere from five to fifteen guests for Christmas Eve dinner because it was also Caesar's birthday. Nellie worked over the turkeys

Nellie and Maggie

and roasts and I finished three apple pies in time to start on my biggest project to date: Caesar's layered birthday cake with inches of fluffy frosting.

"Here comes B.G. Airways!" someone shouted and the hubbub began. Nellie and I stayed in the kitchen and saw Don run past as he dashed for the jeep. Secret smiles and mysterious looks were exchanged all around.

But the mood shifted when the jeep got back from the airstrip.

"They didn't come," Don said, unloading bags of flour and cartons of canned goods where we worked in the kitchen. He was referring to our Christmas presents. We had chosen a plastic swimming pool for little Chris, cartoon films for Peter and Luke.

"Maybe there'll be an extra plane today," I offered hopefully. And there was. But it, too, failed to disgorge our treasures. "Well, at least we have plenty of food for everyone," I said, watching while cartons of canned goods from the second plane were piled against the kitchen wall.

By late afternoon the path to the outside bathroom saw serious traffic as we all hurried to shower before the guests arrived. Pixie and Don were still putting final touches on the 'tree', which was little more than a savannah bush.

"I think this is the last day I'll be able to wedge myself into these frontier pants," I remarked to Don as we finished dressing in our little bedroom. "There aren't any rubber bands big enough any more to hold the waist together."

The sound of the jeep bringing Nellie's sister, Amy, her husband Ben, and four of their grown children was quickly followed by the lights of another vehicle, harder to hear through the excited chatter. Another sister, Maggie, arrived with her grown son, Louis, and her friend Eric Cossou, the District Commissioner for the Runpununi.

Caesar was in his element. The rum punch he offered

disappeared like the Ireng River in dry season. I ducked into the kitchen to frost the cake and came out to see everyone had found a place at the long table, now almost sagging under its load of turkey, ham, vegetables, rolls, bread, wine, champagne, fruit cake, apple pies, cookies, candies, plum pudding, and hard sauce. It was a merry feast. It was time for The Cake.

When I'd left the kitchen to join the others for dinner, I felt I'd created my first masterpiece. What Mariana now carried in was a naked cake, its frosting "de-fluffed" by the heat of 49 candles. Again, I was the object of fun.

"Keep trying, Yan," Caesar chuckled. "We'll make a pastry chef out of you yet."

It was two a.m. before most of the guests climbed back into their jeeps and trucks.

"Watch out for the ant hills," Caesar shouted after each driver. Even in the bright moonlight it would be hard to make out the 5-foot anthills pock-marking the savannah. "See you Old Year's Night," he added.

"Ant hills!" Don and I shook our heads as we ducked back under the front arbor.

Peter and Luke pleaded with their parents to go right into the opening of presents. But we adults were all exhausted and fell into bed right away.

"Happy Fourth of July," I mumbled as the next morning dawned sticky and hot. "It sure doesn't seem like Christmas to me."

But it soon did. Peter and Luke dove into their toys and books, Caesar and Nellie beamed as Pixie put on her pretty gold bracelet, and Don was gleeful as he held up the fishing rod and reel I'd given him.

I got sewing baskets. Four of them. We all laughed at that.

Luke soon tired of the little tanks that shot sparks and decided to go out onto the savannah in search of something more exciting. "Think I'll go look for that keebeehee I saw out there the other day," he called back to us. Peter followed and their Indian friend Phillip shadowed them as usual.

"He's going to look for *what*?" I exclaimed.

"A keebeehee," Nellie offered. "It's a kind of raccoon that makes a lovely pet."

Someone should have notified the keebeehee of that description. Within minutes all was chaos.

"Mom! Mom!" Peter shouted as he ran toward the house. "Luke's hurt!"

We all ran to the front door as Luke limped and hopped towards us, blood streaming down his leg. It was badly torn in several places. That particular keebeehee did not fancy becoming Luke's pet. Its teeth and claws made the point.

"Come on, son," Nellie said calmly. "Let's get your leg bathed. Fortunately Dr. Talbot will be along later today on his way to Karasabai. Lucky for you."

That was debatable. Luke's pain of a badly torn leg was joined by the pain of a penicillin shot to his bottom and tetanus shot to his arm. "Merry Christmas," he muttered to himself later as he went back to the toy tanks and their sparks.

For the next few days Don flew off to recruit and organize men for the mining operations at Marquis, the name Don and I chose for our valley and home site. I suggested the name which described the shape of my engagement diamond and Caesar had approved. He said it was easy for the Indians to pronounce. Marquis was fifteen minutes by plane north of Good Hope past Karasabai village, where the Macusi Indians lived. The men Don hired would assemble barges under Harry Hart's direction. These would hold the mining equipment on the Ireng River, which flowed past

Janet Haack

our home site. The construction of our house had taken a back seat to the mining start-up. So far, it was only a sketch and some ideas on a scratchpad.

Nellie offered me the use of her sewing machine so that I could start on my maternity wardrobe and baby clothes. One thing Georgetown had offered was a great choice of fabrics and patterns. The machine was a treadle—the generator for electricity at Good Hope only came on at night—but I got the hang of it and passed the hours Don was away by creating my "tents" and tiny batiste shirts and sleep wear for our baby.

With only a couple of days left in 1955, Don offered to fly me up to Marquis to choose the house site. We invited Pixie to fly along and she suggested a "picnic."

"That's a great idea," Don exclaimed.

"There's a wonderful spot just a little bit north of your place called Karona Falls," Pixie continued. "We'll ask Harry to come along," she said, referring to her cousin, our foreman.

We packed a picnic lunch, to include a couple of gallons of lemonade, and were soon in the air for the fifteen-minute flight to Marquis.

As we settled down on our own airstrip and climbed down from the plane, I marveled at what a beautiful little valley we would live in. Enclosed on three sides by low forested mountains and on the fourth by the Ireng River, Marquis felt not so much isolated as safe. On the other side of the Ireng was Brazil.

"Let's go!" urged Pixie, grabbing the shotgun and a gallon of lemonade. Harry led the way and I followed Pixie. Don took up the rear.

Somehow they had all neglected to tell me that Karona Falls was a seven-mile hike upriver. After a couple of miles and hearing "just over that small green hill up ahead" several times, I was ready for a break. Just then, Pixie tripped over a log and let out a cry. I looked down where she lay sprawled and saw blood flowing from her hand. She had smashed her finger between the gun butt and a rock. Suddenly I felt very, very faint and sat down on another rock nearby. I watched Pixie wrap her finger in a handkerchief.

"Maybe we'd better turn back here," I offered, hopefully.

But Pixie would have none of it. A couple of minutes later, hand over her head, she hopped up and was back on the path. We stopped at a little creek meandering its way toward the Ireng, swam a bit, ate our lunch, and battled the cabourri flies.

We never did make it that day to Karona Falls. We needed to figure in enough time for a flight to be concluded by dusk, which in that area usually came at six p.m.

"It was a marvelous picnic," Pixie exclaimed to her mother on our return. Nellie snipped away loose skin from her daughter's mangled finger and dressed it in clean bandages. Nothing seemed to faze this woman, I thought. *I hope I can become such a mother.*

On Old Year's Night, as the locals called it, seven of us clambered onto the jeep for the ride to Perara, Amy and Ben Hart's ranch twenty miles south of Good Hope. Caesar followed what he called a road, and I was making fun of his jeep.

"I know," he called over the noise of engine and rough road. "It only has the bare essentials."

"An ignition would be nice," I gasped, hanging onto the front seat and side handle so as not to be dislodged. "Every time we have to run further and push harder. Pretty soon I'm going to have to drop out! And no brakes? No gas, oil, or temperature guages?"

We pulled into Perara's "yard" and Caesar quickly

shifted into first gear, switched off the ignition, and abruptly let up on the clutch.

"You see, Yan. We stopped!" he said triumphantly as I pushed back from the dashboard.

We all took turns showering off the dust in Perara's bathhouse and put on fresh cotton dresses and sport shirts. After a cup of tea, some impatient soul yelled, "Let's go," and we were off on another, shorter, hair-raising ride toward Lethem, a small government outpost in the middle of nowhere.

The party was in full swing at Uncle Teddy's Guesthouse. Teddy, another Melville, was brother to Nellie, Amy, and Maggie. A four-piece band was far past sobriety and the guests were close behind. We danced and ate until the wee hours of 1956 and somehow made it back to Perara and our hammocks, without hitting any anthills along the way.

Young Ben and Elmo Hart, Ben and Amy's sons, had made big plans for fishing on New Year's Day. A few yards from the house, Perara Creek teemed with fish. I looked for the rods and reels.

"Oh no, Jan," Elmo directed. "We set dynamite charges on the creek bottom and when the water calms after the explosion, everyone jumps in and grabs a stunned fish." A big *boom* caught my attention and I turned to see Nellie and Pixie, short black hair shining in the sun, bobbing and laughing as they tossed their catches into the boat. I slid into the water and swam toward a nearby fish.

"A-a-gh!" I exclaimed, letting go instantly of the cold and wriggling slippery fish. "I think I'll just watch the rest of you."

Much of daily life was like that: our entertainment involved hunting, fishing, gathering food for the table. On my birthday in January Pixie suggested a quail hunt. I gamely started off with them, but my increased bulk made it hard to keep up. Don annoyingly referred to me as "heavy with colt" and insisted that these activities would be good for me. I'd rather be in a hammock with a good book—or even a bad one—but Pixie and Don would keep after me until I relented.

I felt that Pixie had delusions of grandeur as far as pigeons, quail, and other edible wildlife went. An hour's tramp in the savannah yielded five quail that day, one apiece for Nellie, Caesar, Pixie, Don, and me. Luckily the boys were back at school. And fortunately there was plenty of rice, beans, and farine to fill in the empty spaces around the bony quail bites. *Happy birthday, me.*

"How about a trip down to Gomes' tomorrow," Caesar asked at breakfast a few days later. Now here was a plan I could go for. A scenic ride down the Ireng in a motor boat to visit the nearest store. "We can do some fishing on the way—this time with rod and reel, Yan," he winked at me.

"Great idea," Don said. "My men up at Marquis need some more coffee and beans, and I don't plan a trip to Georgetown for a while. Lord knows I don't want to give them any reason to quit. Getting set up takes so darned long," he said, sounding dejected.

"When you do everything from scratch, it does," Caesar replied. "You haven't an easy task, remember, setting up far from civilization. Don't get discouraged. Nellie and I think you've done very well. Come on, now, let's not waste any more time."

Nellie fetched long sleeve shirts and long pants for four-year-old Christopher. "There'll be plenty of cabourri flies on the river," she warned. "You'd better take a hat and scarf, Jan."

"And bring a good supply of sheer pins for the motor,"

Caesar called to Don. With years of experience, Caesar knew he could not find *all* the channels in the ever-changing river, though with the river as low as it was he could miss most of the rocks.

It was a grand ride downstream. Huge turtles basked along the riverbanks and brilliant macaws scattered from the treetops at the sound of our motor.

"Guess we didn't need these after all," Don said, holding up a fistful of sheer pins as he got out of the boat and pulled it up on the bank.

"Hang onto them," Caesar cautioned. "It's the trip back up the river where we may need them all."

We climbed the high bank of the Brazilian side to the flat land covered in brush. Gomes' one room store sat alone in a small cleared area. It was dark inside the mud hut, but I could make out the huge sacks on the hard mud floor: dried beans, brown sugar—syrup oozing through the burlap—flour, farine, coffee. The narrow shelves sagged with the weight of dusty bottles of Vaseline hair oil, tonics, tins of butter, and bolts of gaudy cotton prints.

The men got right into it, ordering supplies for home and campsite, talking cattle prices and politics. Pixie, Nellie, Christopher and I sat at the back of the room on lumpy sacks. We sipped strong black Brazilian coffee heavily laced with sugar from Gomes' tiny cups. A pig ambled in one door and out the other. Cats were everywhere.

I bought some narrow satin ribbon to use for our baby's layette. Feeling pleased that at least I'd made a purchase, I followed the others back down the slippery mud bank and into the boat.

Caesar had been right, again. Several times on the return trip the strong current carried our boat where we most certainly didn't want to go—and there went a sheer pin. Rocks appeared everywhere and our supply of sheer pins dwindled rapidly.

At an open spot on the riverbank, Caesar pulled up the boat and announced it was time to fish. Nellie was delighted and first out of the boat. She chose her spot on the riverbank and expertly cast her line into the water. Time after time, she reeled in lukananis and arawhannas. She laughed and called out as she splashed, fully-clothed, into the river with her net. Part of her joy must have been contemplating something other than dried beef and farine for dinner that night.

As I sat on the bank and watched her skillfully put her fish on a stringer, I marveled at the adaptability of this woman. *How lucky I am to have her for my role model.*

In just over two months I'd seen Nellie as nurse, hostess, midwife, chef, companion, seamstress, handyman, and now fisherwoman. Who better could teach me how to love the life we now had?

As I watched the others from my seat on the riverbank, I wondered how she managed such equilibrium. She never knew if there would be five or twenty-five for noonday dinner on mail plane day. One Sunday fourteen young Brazilian students had dropped by unannounced just before noon. Resting from their hike, they'd sprawled in the Berbice chairs which lined the long front gallery of the house.

"Why, you don't even *know* them!" I said with exasperation as I followed Nellie out to the kitchen.

Nellie smiled. "Here, Jan," she said, handing me a pitcher. "You can make the lemonade."

Finally, even Nellie was tired from hauling in her catch. Her stringer was full while Caesar and Don's held just a few each. We all slid back down the bank and into the boat, ready to dodge rocks and get home with a few sheer pins left over.

Janet Haack

As I sat in the boat, I looked at Nellie still dripping wet, and thought of the day she and I had washed clothes together in the Ireng. Mariana, Nellie's sole source of help in the house was in bed with an attack of reoccurring malaria. I had headed to the bathhouse to suds out a few clothes in a basin there when I spotted Nellie, weighed down with a bag of laundry, headed for the river.

"You're not going to do *our* wash!" I called after her. But there was determination in her step as she continued down the path. "At least not without me!" I added.

I thought Nellie would die laughing at the sight of me as I squatted on a rock in the Ireng and pounded away at our clothes spread on a flat rock beside me.

"How's this for an endless water supply?" she shouted, as she slid off *her* rock, pulling her clothes off as she went. She splashed around, washing both her clothes and herself. "You can't do this with your fancy washing machines," she laughed.

Suddenly two little Indian girls appeared on the riverbank to watch our fun. Nellie recognized them and, as we hung our clothes on the fence to dry, spoke rapidly to them in a strange language. They listened in silence. That day Neka and Pauline became part of the Good Hope household.

"Where are the Whiz Kids," Don asked a few days later. We had dubbed them that because, although Nellie spoke the Macusi language well, neither Pauline nor Neka seemed to understand that any better than our sign language. Pauline constantly lugged a baby sister along on her hip and occasionally dropped her, much to Nellie's and my consternation. Neka was never disturbed by this. She would pick the crying baby up and plant her back on Pauline's hip.

"Nellie sent Neka out to the garden to get some onions for lunch," I replied to Don's question. "I saw her point to an onion, the garden, then to Neka, saying, I think, the Macusi words for 'go' and 'bring'."

Twenty minutes later I was out in the kitchen as Nellie wondered aloud that Neka was still not back.

"I'll go find her," I offered. And there she was, still standing and looking at the garden, thoroughly puzzled. *What part of the sign language or Macusi did she not understand?* I pulled a couple of onions from the garden and took Neka by the hand. I led her back to the kitchen.

That night after dinner, Don and I were writing letters to our families. "You know, you've come a long way in a short time," he mused, stuffing his epistle in an envelope and licking the flap. "I just described to Mom and Dad the menagerie that lives in our bedroom and told them you have become quite the pioneer."

"Yeah. I'm way past lizards," I said wryly, finishing my own description of life at Good Hope in the letter to my parents. "I now occupy a bedroom with lizards, mice brought in by the cat, some arriving on their own, and a monstrous toad which has taken up residence under my bed. It's all the jolly good fun you promised me it would be."

That night I groaned as the noise of squealing mice reached its zenith. "Can't you stop this ruckus?" I pleaded. But Don was as reluctant to put his feet on the floor from his hammock as I was to get out of bed. We never knew when a new "tenant" might have arrived.

5

Adventures Before Children

I was flying in to Georgetown, always by B.G. Airways, for doctor check-ups every four weeks, now. Don was flying our small plane up to Marquis almost every day to supervise the mining operations, plan for the first load of equipment coming in, and start the construction of our house. Our "damnedmudhut," as my father was calling it, would be ready, if not in time for our baby's arrival, at least soon afterward.

On my February jaunt to Georgetown, the DC-3 took off from Good Hope and headed east toward Tiny and Connie McTurk's ranch, Karanambo. Tiny must have radioed down to B.G Airways that he had cargo to ship to Georgetown. I'd heard a lot about the McTurk's though I hadn't met them. I recognized Tiny at once as the plane rolled to a stop on his airstrip. A battered khaki hat shielded his chiseled, weather beaten face as he poked his head in the door of the plane.

"Got room for a crate full of Tiger Cat?" he called up front to the pilot.

"Tiger Cat?" I reacted immediately. "Where? How old is it? Is it for sale? Where are you sending it? Could I buy it?" The questions tumbled over each other.

"Buy it?" He grinned. "Well, I was sending 'im to the

zoo in Georgetown, but you kin have 'im if you want 'im."
This could be the perfect mate for Chibi.

I introduced myself to Tiny and we chatted as the Karanambo mail was unloaded. He told me some natives had caught the Tiger Cat (the smallest member of the Ocelot family)and brought it to his house days earlier.

"Had quite a time too, they did. He's a few months old, I figger. You sure you still want 'im?"

Sight unseen, I wanted him. I stopped and peered into the dark crate as the plane taxied for take-off. I was greeted with a spit and a hiss. Rebuffed, I made it back to my bucket seat and strapped myself in. Flying over the solid green floor between the savannah and Georgetown, I realized the foolishness of my impulse. *How will I keep this darned thing in the hotel? And at Good Hope? Don will disown me if I bring him a tiger cat instead of the Gorgonzola cheese I promised him.*

It took some convincing to get a couple of bellboys to bring the crate up to my room at the Woodbine. Mac Wiltshire always gave me our same room when I came into town. It hadn't changed. I lay down on one of the beds to contemplate the situation. The little cat seemed more afraid of me than I of him. *I just need to show him I'm not going to hurt him. After all, he isn't much bigger than a full grown house cat.*

I got up, closed the door and windows to the veranda, opened the front of the crate, and stood back. A streak of fur zipped under the bed. Once again, I got down on my knees to peer into his dark hiding place in the corner. I spent an hour on the floor as we faced off each other. But no amount of gentle tones or friendly words would evoke more than a snarl and a spit. *Well, at least it doesn't want to come near me, so I don't need to worry about being attacked.*

After dinner I managed to corral Tigger, as I'd named him, in the space under the built-in dressing table. I barricaded the opening with a suitcase, the empty crate, and a chair. My "goodnight/sleep tight" was met with the usual hiss/spit.

The room was stifling. I didn't dare open the door or windows to the veranda for fear Tigger would escape. I lay under the mosquito netting, wishing it had been designed to hold out more than insects. Listening for every sound of movement, the only thing I could hear was my heart pounding in my ears. *What in the world was I thinking? Thinking?*

After dressing next morning, I pulled the barricade away from Tigger's space under the dressing table. He was still there. His beautifully marked face held huge dark eyes, trained on mine. He didn't blink and continued to crouch in the corner, defiant. I tried a few more soft soothing words, put the barricades back in place, then slipped out the door to go down to breakfast.

I brought some scraps of food back up to the room and found a broom, mop, bucket, and cleaning cloths outside the door. Under no circumstances would the maid go in *that* room. The Amerindians took the animals of the jungle more or less in their stride. But Georgetown was inhabited by blacks and East Indians, neither of which had any use for wild animals. Blacks especially cultivated an irrational fear of them. I'm surprised the maid even showed up at the hotel, I thought, as I swept the floor and cleaned the sink.

On the way back from my doctor's visit that afternoon, I stopped to pick up some fresh meat for Tigger. I'd put water down in a small bowl the cook had given me from the hotel kitchen, but wasn't sure my new "pet" would even come near it.

Opening the door with a friendly, "Here, Tigger. Come, Tigger," I put the meat down on the floor of his open cage and took down the barricades. For the rest of the afternoon it was "nice baby," "Here little Tigger," "Come on little one." He could not be persuaded.

Well I've gotten myself into this mess, and I'd better hurry up and find a solution. It finally hit me— I'd call Louis Chung, a friend of ours who owned a tropical fish business and had a warehouse up at Atkinson Field. His wife, Winnie, was our company secretary. Surely Louis could take Tigger for a while and maybe even find a home for him.

"Sure Jan," Louis said over the phone when I posed the question. "No trouble."

I breathed a huge sigh of relief, then went back upstairs to the room, hoping to find Tigger in the cage licking his lips. No such luck. This was one stubborn tiger cat. And now he was back under the bed in the corner, his vocabulary still the same: "Hiss-spit."

I was to fly to Orinduick next day, where Don would meet the plane and take me back to Good Hope. Somehow I needed to get Tigger back in the cage. I needed help.

"Mama," I said over the phone. I was using the pet name for Mrs. Mittelhouser who owned the boarding house where all Gorinskys stayed while in Georgetown. "I need to speak to Peter or Luke. I need some help with a tiger cat in my hotel room."

Surely she thought I was crazy, but Mama took most things in stride and she called Peter to the phone anyway.

"Peter, I have this little tiger cat in my room at the Woodbine, and I can't get near him no matter what I do. I'm leaving tomorrow to go back to Good Hope and Louis Chung has offered to keep him up at Atkinson. But he's out of his cage, and I have to catch him. He's not very friendly," I finished in grand understatement.

Now what 14-year-old who loves animals would not rise to that challenge? Within half an hour, both boys showed up on their bicycles, left them in the driveway and bolted up the stairs.

"Don't worry, Jan," Peter said confidently, pulling the blanket off the foot of my bed. "We'll get him."

I was not only dubious, I was scared. I remembered only too clearly the keebeehee incident in the bush and all Luke's blood that was lost. But after much scrambling and snarling, defeated Tigger was caged, and the triumphant boys, unscathed.

"All in a day's work," Peter smiled. "Though I'm not sure it did much for Tigger's acceptance of humans."

That made me sad, but I did look forward to a full night's sleep that night.

I had not a shred of regret about leaving Tigger behind next morning when the DC-3 took off. My mood lightened, knowing that when he met the plane, Don would not be the wiser for my foolishness. Everything was nicely taken care of.

"Hi, Hon!" Don called as he strode towards me from the shade of our plane wing "Where is he?"

"Where's who?" I asked, caught completely off balance.

"Our new Tiger Cat, silly. Tiny McTurk was over at Good Hope yesterday and told us all about it."

Now what do I do?

Uh. . . yeah. Well…I thought I'd have Louis Chung ship him up by the next plane going to Good Hope," I smiled. "I've named him Tigger, but he's not very friendly," I finished, using my new favorite understatement.

Hastily I scribbled a note to Louis, redirecting his efforts, and gave it to the pilot to take back down to Atkinson Field. This was much against my good judgment, but Don, and later Pixie, were so enthusiastic about taming Tigger, I decided it was a good idea after all.

"When you bring Chibi down from the 'States," Pixie mused later that day, "she'll have a husband. And you and

Don can raise little Chibi's!"

I tried to prepare them. "This cat is already wild! He does not like humans!"

"All we'll need is a little patience," Don observed. "I'm sure we can tame him. It takes time, you know, Hon."

I smiled.

Ten days later, Tigger arrived at Good Hope and Don lugged the cage into our bedroom and undid the latch.

"Come on, kitty, let's see what you look like."

Don't! Don't put your hand in there!" I yelled. Tigger was already in the midst of his repertoire of snarls and hisses. Don retreated.

"We'll leave him alone for a while. Let him get used to the place," he suggested—wisely, I thought.

While we ignored him, Tigger stayed in the corner of our room, his huge dark and beautiful eyes following our every move. Again, we kept our windows and doors closed so he couldn't leave the room. That night the room was stale and hot and sleep was impossible. I lay on my bed staring far up to the grass peak of the roof. (For better air circulation, walls in these tropical houses did not have a ceiling connecting them. They served merely as partitions.) I knew Don wasn't asleep either.

"See what I meant about his personality?" I whispered across to his hammock. Pixie's room was on the other side of the wall and I didn't want to wake her.

"I'm not giving up yet," Don whispered back. "He'll have to make friends sometime."

I checked the mosquito netting around the mattress to make sure it was secure. Tigger crouched noiselessly in his corner.

Next morning, Don and I were coming back through the front gallery after breakfast, when suddenly we saw Tigger peering round the frame of our bedroom door which we'd closed but forgotten to latch. At the sight and sound of us, he streaked up and out the front window of the gallery.

Without hesitation, Don and Pixie were after him. I lumbered after them, half-heartedly. Secretly I hoped Tigger would escape.

"There he goes!" yelled Pixie. "There! Under that big bush!" They were yards ahead of me, but I ran up panting as they circled the bush, cornering Tigger.

"I've got him!" Don cried triumphantly, as he grabbed for Tigger. But Tigger grabbed with teeth and claws at the same time, and Don's hand was the nearest target.

Together Pixie and Don wrestled Tigger back to the house.

"Get those leather gloves of yours, Jan," he ordered. "You're going to hold this guy, and I'm going to clip those damned claws of his." *Now I know what those gloves I brought are for!*

I really didn't like this situation anymore. Here was a wild animal snatched out his habitat by humans and was now being subdued in their interest of having a pet. While Don clipped his claws, I held Tigger who now was surprisingly quiet.

Nellie ministered to Don's hand, saying little. If she disapproved, she didn't say so. It was a silence born of wisdom.

Tigger snarled from his corner for several days, waiting for another opportunity to escape. Which he did. Pixie and I hunted through swamps and fields for him. It was a feeble search. Nellie looked relieved at the loss of her unfriendly boarder and even Don, on his return from the mine site, did not bemoan Tigger's escape.

I had one more month left for adventure before my increasing bulk made me more of a liability than an eager companion. I flew with Don in our plane several times a week, sometimes to Marquis, sometimes to Lethem. One morning Don and Caesar asked me if I'd like to go along on their duck hunt next day.

"It'll be fun once we get going," Don urged, seeing my grimace at the thought of a 4:00 a.m. rising.

So, I was along for the ride when Caesar pointed the jeep lights toward the open savannah in the darkness the next morning. Phillip, Peter's little Indian friend and Good Hope's general factotum, bounced along in the rear of the jeep. He would make a good duck-chaser.

In the rainy season the lowlands collect water to become small freshwater lakes, perfect resting spots for the "Wississee" and Teal ducks. Small and fast, the Wississee make for a great hunt as well as a good meal. When the rains subside, the lakes get smaller and the ducks concentrate on those that are still good size.

Caesar chose one lake an hour's ride from Good Hope. For a more effective hunt, we separated: Don and I on the far side of the lake, Caesar and Phillip nearer the jeep. As we waded and crouched low, Don kept telling me to make myself invisible.

That'll be a good trick in my condition. I yanked at the duck bag, which had once again slipped below my swollen belly.

"Let's wade across here," Don directed when we reached a shallow edge on the way to the opposite side of the lake. "It'll save us a mile of walking."

We slogged on.

"I hope we don't disturb the caimans," he commented, mostly to himself.

"Oh, you're *so* funny," I replied. "Well, I don't scare that easily." I knew he and Caesar wouldn't actually put me in harm's way.

"Good girl," he grinned.

We'd reached the other side and he raised his gun as

a flock of ducks flew over, whistling their distinctive call. Pow! A duck fell into the water a few yards from us. Don started for it, when a large dark form slithered out and closed its powerful jaws on the hapless duck. We watched in silence.

"You won't get me back in that water again!" I croaked, when I'd half recovered from my shock. "We're walking *around* if it takes the rest of the day!"

Not surprisingly, he agreed. After we'd bagged ten ducks, Don took the load and we started back, on land. My eyes took in everything that might turn out to be a caiman, but we never saw another one. Nonetheless, I stayed as close behind Don as my protrusion would allow, halving, I hoped, my chances of being eaten.

Nellie was a happy woman when she saw the load of ducks we brought back. I recounted our sighting of the caiman and she threw Caesar a disapproving glance.

"I think it's time Jan stayed closer to home, now. This was quite an adventure, but it should be her last for a while." She looked for my consent.

I loved being a superwoman, proving to all that, pregnant or not, American lady or not, I could "run with the boys." Lately I had felt wisdom coming with motherhood, thank heavens, and I nodded at Nellie.

"I know. The baby's due in early April. I guess I should make plans to go to town on the next plane to Good Hope. That will give me a couple of weeks to get everything ready."

I looked at Don and both of us realized our life was about to make a big change. I was reluctant to leave the dry open savannahs to go in to the hot humid city. However, I did have to smile as I took my slim skirts and small-waisted dresses from the trunk later in the week and packed them in the suitcase for town.

"I'll be down about the first of April, Hon," Don said, helping me up the ladder and into the DC-3 that Friday. It was a tough parting. We realized that when we were together next, someone quite a bit smaller would be in command.

6

Motherhood

In Georgetown the driver dropped me off in front of Pam Wheating's huge white frame house across from the Parade Ground. Pam had invited me to stay with her until Don came down to town from the interior. Convenient location, I thought, looking next door at Mercy Hospital. *You can come any time now, baby Haack. I have doctors within hailing distance.*

"You are in time for tea!" Pam reached out to give me a hug. "I am so happy to have you here and you need not worry about being a nuisance. I'll see to it that you have everything in readiness for your child's arrival." Pam was taking charge and I was glad of it. Her dark eyes flashed as she chattered away while the servant came and went with tea, little sandwiches, and tiny cakes.

"Now, do not get up in the morning, Jan, please," she instructed. "It will ruin everything. Beryl will bring you your breakfast in bed and you must take your time. Mornings are just beastly around here. Tom is impossible. He storms around wanting this and that and the children... well, it is just a zoo. It will be *much* better if you stay out of the way." It was more than a suggestion.

Pam showed me to "my" room looking out over the

Parade Ground across the street. The room was sunny and spacious with a huge bed draped in yards of white mosquito netting. The windows, framed outside by fuschia bouganvillea, were open to the breeze coming across the open ground. *And I have to stay in bed to eat breakfast? That'll be tough!*

Beryl, the maid, rapped softly on my door next morning. I called for her to come in and watched as she bustled about the room a little before bringing my breakfast tray to the bed and setting it on my knees. I thanked her as casually as I knew how, trying to leave the impression that I had a servant serve me breakfast in bed all the days of my life. I ate my fruit and porridge and toast as slowly as I could manage, hearing little of the bedlam that Pam had described the previous day. Soon I heard Tom's car pull away and decided it was safe to dress and appear downstairs.

Pam greeted me with a cheery good morning. Apparently, my timing coincided with her schedule.

"Now this morning, I want you to walk over to the hospital and ask to see the head maternity nurse," Pam instructed. "She will tell you what you need to bring to the hospital with you when the time comes. I will do my errands and see you at lunch. "Ta," she called, heading for the kitchen.

I headed out the front door and down the steps, turning left at the end of the front walk. The sunshine was brilliant, the gardens lush, and I was happy in my expectation of imminent motherhood. I crossed the courtyard behind the main building and found the new maternity wing. Mercy was a Catholic hospital run by nuns from the United States. A huge white wooden structure, it gleamed amongst the riot of color from its surrounding gardens.

A dark-skinned woman in a crisp white uniform sat behind the desk in the second floor office. The door was

Janet Haack

Mercy Hospital—Georgetown

open and I knocked timidly on the frame to catch her attention. She looked up and beckoned to come in.

"Good Morning. How can I help you?"

I introduced myself and told her I was a patient of Dr. Lyder's. "I thought you might give me some idea of what I'm expected to bring with me when I come for the birth of our baby," I ventured.

"Of course," she replied. "Do you have paper and a pencil? You'll never be able to remember it all," she announced with a smile. Surprised that I would need it, I took a pen and little notebook from my purse.

"Let's see. . . you will need diapers and receiving blankets, of course, and shirts for the baby, belly-bands, alcohol, Limacol for your back rubs, and some "spirits" in case you have any fainting spells. You will want several nightgowns and under clothing for yourself. If you take aspirin, please bring it with you and do arrange to have yours and the baby's laundry done while you're here. Yes, I think that's all."

"The diapers, receiving blankets, and shirts aren't a problem," I told Pam later at lunch. And I'll pick up some Limacol and smelling salts at Booker's tomorrow. But what in the world are 'belly bands'?"

Pam chuckled. "Don't worry. I'll have my maid tear some strips of old sheeting. The nurses will use it to protect the baby's navel." This world was getting newer and newer to me.

Don flew into town the second week in April and I left the luxury of Pam's house to join him at the Woodbine until our baby's arrival, which was now overdue. Dr. Lyder asked me to come for an X-ray because the baby did not seem to be in the correct position. I waited while the film developed and then met him in his office.

"What we have here is a frank breach," he said

unceremoniously. "It's no wonder you've had to sit up straighter and straighter. The baby's head is under one side of your ribs and feet straight up under the other side. I think we'll have to do a Caesarian. Come, I want you to meet our chief surgeon, Dr. Jewel."

Suddenly I was scared. Things were definitely not going according to my plan.

"Buck up, Hon," Don coached, squeezing my arm as we left the hospital. I had seen Dr. Jewel, the head surgeon at Mercy Hospital before calling Don at the hotel to come get me. The baby's delivery was scheduled for the next day.

"Let's just be glad you got to town in plenty of time and didn't stay to have the baby in the Rupununi like everyone was encouraging you to do."

Thank God for some common sense.

Diana Lynn was born at 8:00 a.m. the next morning. Though taken, her footprints were unnecessary for identification. She was the only white baby in the nursery. Chinese, East Indian, African and mixtures of all these—it was a colorful nursery.

"She's pretty cute for such a cheap baby," Don offered when I woke up. "What a bargain for sixty dollars. Wait 'til you see her! Sister Generosa let me carry her from the delivery room to the nursery," he grinned, obviously feeling very special.

Just then the nurse brought in our baby and laid her by my side. I unwrapped the blanket. "She's got your feet all right," I said, noting the "size nines" on our otherwise delicate, beautiful, perfect little girl. "She'll make a good duck bag carrier," I murmured and drifted back to sleep.

Don flew back to the interior after a few days to look after the construction of our house and the mining operations. Marie and Pam made daily visits, bringing me edible food.

"This porridge is disgusting," Marie remarked, as she shoveled the bowl's contents into the toilet. "I have brought you some fruit and buns and a box of American cereal," she said, propping me up in the bed and putting a tray of offerings on my now-recovered lap. She did this day after day for the whole week I was there.

One morning after Marie left, I lay in bed watching the matinee performance of two lizards on the wall opposite the bed. Sister Generosa, the dear, humorous nun I'd come to love, rushed into the room.

"The Bishop is here to see you, Mrs. Haack," she announced breathlessly. I noticed the bustle in the hallway.

"The Bishop?" I repeated. "Oh my goodness! Don flew him around the interior last month and made him sit on a sack of flour! And he's here to see me?" I quickly ran a comb through my hair and managed to sit up in bed so that Sister Generosa could plump the pillows behind me and make me presentable.

"This is such an *honor*!" she exclaimed as she turned to escort the Catholic Bishop of the West Indies into my room.

Tall and distinguished, Bishop Gilley strode into the room. In his white cassock, this fine-looking man was a most compelling figure.

"Good morning, Mrs. Haack," he said. How nice to see you looking so well." His eyes fixed on mine and he was oblivious to the many dark faces peeping around the doorjamb.

This is, indeed, an event!

"I appreciate your taking your time to come see me," I replied. "It has been a long time since I saw you last. Don is still embarrassed that you had to sit on that bag of flour the day he flew you into Karasabai."

"Not at all, not at all," the Bishop smiled. "I was glad not to have gone by foot. It would have taken a full day."

The two of us chatted pleasantly for another few minutes before he stepped back and said he must leave. I thanked him again for coming, still feeling awkward to have such a distinguished visitor. From the reaction of Sister Generosa and heightened atmosphere in the maternity ward, I knew I had been honored.

Marie and Pam both descended on me that evening.

"The Bishop!" they said almost in unison. "You *did* ask him to bless the baby, didn't you?" Pam continued. My face betrayed my faux pas. "Oh, Jan!" Their consternation covered me like cold water from a bucket.

What must Bishop Gilley think?

I was still worried next day when I bade Sister Generosa and the other nurses in the ward goodbye. I was grateful to them for their care, advice, and loving patience. And for the beautiful blue-eyed daughter placed in my arms as I left.

Pam's gray Citroen pulled up in the courtyard to deliver me to the Woodbine for a few days before my return to the Rupununi. She offered to have me come back to the house but I had declined, convinced they should be spared the presence of a nervous new mother and crying baby.

Tucked into her padded, quilted, beribboned basket, Diana slept through most of the bumpy ride to Atkinson Field the next Friday. But all planes were delayed that morning and I watched helplessly while she voiced outrage at the conditions of travel to her new home. Fortunately, she could still eat, and I was the only starving one to arrive at Good Hope late in the afternoon.

Caesar and Don were waiting with the jeep at the airstrip and we all rushed our fair skinned baby to the shade and cool of the house.

Nellie was ecstatic. "Oh Jan, I was hoping it would be a girl! She is so beautiful."

Nellie took the other end of the fancy basket and

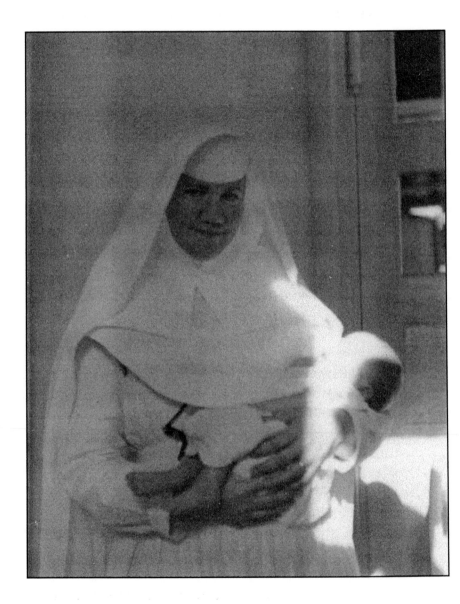

Sister Generosa holding Diana Lynn

together we toted it to the prescribed place in front of the open "frangipani window" of our room.

"It will be nice and cool for her here." We lifted the basket and placed it across the long wooden arms of the Berbice chair.

"How's the house coming?" I asked Don that evening as we walked through the grove of citrus trees on the way to the bathhouse. I turned on the overhead shower while he filled the enamel basin with water to shave.

"Oh hell," he muttered. "You'd think those guys had never built a house the way things are going. It'll be another month or six weeks before we can move in."

Under Harry's direction, the men were making mud blocks in a wooden frame. They had to dig the clay and then trample it with water and grass to the right consistency, before ladling it into the wooden frames for drying.

As six weeks stretched into seven with no completion date set, I decided to make a quick trip back to the 'States so Don's parents and mine could see their new grandchild.

"You'll be glad of the brief respite!" I laughed to Nellie as I told her of my plan. Diana had been yowling through much of the night, and while Caesar and Nellie protested that it bothered them not at all, I was convinced everyone was as sleepless as I when I lay listening for her every breath. Don and I took turns carrying her out to the airstrip on the savannah and back again so the others could sleep. The moonlight lit our way and the sky was bright with stars most of those nights.

I found out much later that both Caesar and Nellie lay in bed thinking I'd never return once I'd tasted life the 'States again.

"I don't see how we can take all that stuff!" Don complained, eyeing the paraphernalia I'd loaded into the jeep for the ride to our Grasshopper at the airstrip.

"It all has to go," I replied with a sigh. "From Georgetown to Michigan is a lot of diapers." With an overnight in Trinidad required to get Diana a passport and stops at both San Juan and New York, it would be a long trip.

I climbed into the small space left in the back seat of our plane, and Don handed Diana in to me. She lay lengthwise along my lap, her little head grazing the back of the pilot seat. The noise of the engine soon lulled her to sleep.

This was not first class travel. A smelly gasoline funnel threatened to fall over my right shoulder, and the canvas bag of emergency rations hung over my left. I was grateful when we arrived two hours later at Atkinson Field. But that was just the beginning. I would be on my own for the rest of the journey.

Somehow it was accomplished. As anyone who has done it knows, traveling with an infant is an endurance test. Even Diana looked disgruntled in her first passport photo, taken in Trinidad.

Having objected to Guyana Airways lack of punctuality, she now objected to Pan American Airways. Her wailing obliterated all instructions on the use of life jackets and the means of escape in case of "dumping" over the Atlantic. My modesty compelled me to sit in the baggage compartment to nurse her but we both persevered through it all to reach Idlewild airport in New York.

My mother and father met us to accompany their new granddaughter and long lost daughter on the last leg of the journey—to the lap of luxury I'd almost forgotten. Now it was the soft carpeting and lizardless walls that seemed strange. A pediatrician and my doctor pronounced both mother and daughter fit, surprising my parents who were all too cognizant of the "poor" conditions under which we lived in Guyana. I would write only happy descriptions to them, but they read between the lines and had all too fertile imaginations.

The Haack grandparents, along with Don's brother, wife, and four-year-old daughter flew from Milwaukee for a long weekend of chin-chucking and cooing over Diana. I filled them in as best I could on all that had transpired in the last ten months. With built-in baby sitters, I had a grand time visiting old friends from high school and shopping with my sister, who also flew in for the viewing.

But I missed Don terribly and wrote him that now I missed my new life in South America. "I long to be back to our life and our own house at Marquis. This is fun, of course, and I am wined and dined. But it's not 'me' anymore."

He wrote back: "After three days of searching, the diving crews finally located what seems to be a pocket of diamonds. We're moving the barges up to that spot in the Ireng tomorrow. Our house should be finished by mid-July. I miss you." His tone conveyed some doubt that I'd be back.

But I was ready, much to Mother and Dad's despair. "We'll ship the crib down to you," Mother offered, "so at least this precious child will have a decent bed." Visions of Diana sleeping in a hammock once she'd outgrown the fancy basket were worrying my mother sick.

I cabled Don the time of my arrival in Georgetown and could barely contain my excitement when the plane touched down at Atkinson. He wasn't there. Nor was he at the Woodbine when we arrived in the cool of the evening. It was a disappointment, but surely he'd be here the next day. He wasn't. Next morning I found the B.G. Airways' office in town and stormed up the stairs to the radio room.

"Please radio Don Haack at Good Hope and tell him it was *last* Wednesday his wife and daughter arrived here, not *next* Wednesday!" He got that message loud and clear and was in town by that afternoon.

It was a joyous reunion after a three-week separation. He fell madly in love with his daughter, I fell madly back in love with him, and together the three of us shopped for all the things we needed for our new house. Which was, finally, becoming a reality.

7

A House in the Valley

"You *lost* them! Oh, Harry," I wailed, "now we'll be even farther behind."

I was bemoaning Harry's careless handling of my house plans. The *only* copy of them. Before Diana was born and then during her quiet times, I 'd worked painstakingly at Good Hope's dining room table on the simple but adequate design of our house at Marquis.

"Don't make it anything but square, hon," Don urged when I began. The workmen will never be able to figure anything else out." As it was, Harry and his crew must have viewed a house with three bedrooms, living/dining rooms combined, built in kitchen—built *in* the house— and indoor bathroom as the Taj Mahal, square or no. Unlike houses in the Rupununi, ours was to have closets and a pantry. I'd put them in the plan. Now the plan was lost.

"I'm sorry, Jan," Harry looked at the ground, his battered hat hiding his eyes. This was May and we were standing on the airstrip at Marquis where I'd hoped to find progress on our humble abode. Harry looked up. "But they're doing okay without it." This was an afterthought, flung over his shoulder as he turned back to Don, leaving me to watch several pairs of brown feet as they trampled mud and grass in a large pit. Three rows of blocks baked in the unrelenting sun of mid-afternoon.

"I will bring you another set of plans tomorrow, Harry," I called after him. "And I want you to follow them!" I was getting the "little woman" treatment and I was mad! If I was to live in this place, I wanted my house the way I wanted it.

That night I sat hunched over the dining room table at Good Hope and by the light of a kerosene lamp, drew another set of plans for Harry and his crew. I knew every nook and corner in that house and my measurements were exact. If I'd had a copier, of course, I'd have copied them. But surely Harry knew how displeased I'd been and wouldn't lose them again. Don flew the plans up to Marquis next day and delivered them to Harry.

"How're you coming now?" I asked brightly a few days later when Don flew me up to Marquis again. "Did you get the plans I sent up with Don?"

"Uh, yeah," he muttered, looking at the ground *again.*

"Harry. You didn't!" I already knew the answer.

"Lost 'em somewheres," he admitted. "But we're goin' ahead okay. Come and see." The three of us walked toward the mud house which, so far, consisted of walls and the trusses for the roof, not yet in place.

"Got to get that aluminum roof on quick," Harry commented. "If we get a rain, it'll wash the walls away." This gave me something else to worry about.

"What's this opening doing here?" I asked in amazement, looking at the inner wall of our bedroom. "This room is where we dress and sleep, Harry, but the way you've built it, we'll do that in full view of everyone!"

"We'll figure something out, hon, Don said. "At least it provides cross ventilation." I hated that he was siding with Harry all the time.

"Um, Harry, where is the bathroom?" Now it was Don's turn to question and I took certain comfort in *his* discomfort.

"Guess we'll have to add it on, boss," Harry replied. "The men forgot it 'cause they never saw one *inside* a house before. Sorry. It won't take long to make a few more mud blocks. We'll do it right away."

He and Don wandered off down the path to the barracoun, the plain mud building where the workmen tied their hammocks. Dejected, I explored the house that was different from the one I'd envisioned, but now nearly completed. I could hang a curtain over the opening between our bedroom and the living room. Fortunately, they'd placed a row of windows on the outside bedroom wall high enough so we had some privacy there. At least the kitchen was included in the house and Harry had remembered to put the small pantry next to it.

Suddenly there was a great commotion outside.

"Marabunta! Marabunta!" I looked out the kitchen window to where a crew of workers had been clearing around the perimeter of the house. One of the indians ran back and forth, calling to anyone within earshot and pointing at a huge mud nest, easily three feet in diameter, hanging from a tree and swarming with huge angry wasps. Harry and Don rushed back up the path toward the house. Harry was carrying a gas can fixed with a sprayer. The job of clearing for the house, the barracoun, the airstrip and hangar had taken machetes, explosives, gasoline and countless indian hours.

"Stand back!" Harry ordered, spraying the nest with gasoline, drenching it. Quickly he flung a burning match at it.

Boom! The inferno erupted with a roar and after watching it for a few minutes Harry and Don set off down the path to the river. All in a day's work, I mused, turning from the drama outside to the puzzle inside. A few men, including the alarm raiser still stood watching the burning marabunta nest.

The fire burned down quickly. But it had provided such grand entertainment that an encore was certainly called for—at least by one in the audience. The one called Pedro snatched up the gas can and sprayer and pointed it toward the few remaining flames. Within seconds he was on fire, screaming. The other men were on him instantly, throwing him on the ground, beating at the flames with their shirts. Harry and Don were back in a flash. They both looked Pedro over then lead the hapless fellow back to the barracoun to tend to his burns. *Scary.*

"That was a close one," I said to Don an hour or two later as the two of us walked the path from Good Hope airstrip toward the Gorinsky house. "I'm glad the other crewmen were there. I was paralyzed! I can plainly see Harry has his hands full up there at Marquis. I'll try not to get so mad at him about the house plans anymore."

"Cheer up, hon," Don replied. It's not much, but it's all ours," he said referring to our unpredictable house. "Harry will add the bathroom this week and while he's doing it, he'll add a little library room next to it. That'll give us someplace to build a long desk top for the shortwave radio and your typewriter."

We all laughed later at dinner about the chaos of the day. Don reassured Nellie that he and Harry had done a good job of dressing Pedro's burns.

"We'll keep a close eye on him for a few days and let you know if we need you to look at him," Don assured Nellie.

Diana had behaved well while I was gone those few hours. Nellie was happy to have the baby to herself for a

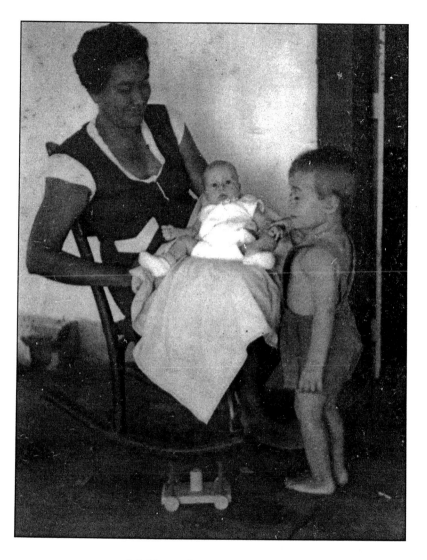

Nellie, Chris and Diney

while. Her own daughter was grown now and away from home and after Pixie, there had been boys, all boys. She loved having a sweet little girl to hold again.

"As far as I'm concerned," Nellie said, "they can keep building that house up there forever! I like having you all here and I'll miss you when you move to Marquis."

The bathroom was added, as promised. Thoughtfully, Harry had placed the windows on the outside shower wall high enough so that we didn't have to bathe in full view of the world. Unfortunately the small eye-level window above the sink gave a charming view of the toilet as well. The shower was spacious, though the drain hole to the outside had been neatly cut out four inches *above* the shower floor. A septic tank was dug a short distance from the house and drainpipes affixed from the base of the toilet. Which was dead level with the septic tank. *Hmmmm.*

Next time I flew to Marquis with Don, the toilet had been elevated to new heights: three steps up to a platform which now allowed for gravity feed to the septic tank. Talk about 'thrones!'

Don was learning patience rapidly.

"Maxim," he said seriously to the Brazilian who had risen to the head of the house building crew, the hole in the shower is for the water to go *out.*" They both stood in the bathroom contemplating the situation.

"Oh, si patron" Maxim replied with a broad grin. "I feex."

He feexed. But the shower floor was slanted *away* from the hole so that water collected in the near corner providing us with a footbath in the shower. Dirt collected there too. *Uh, Maxim. Just one more thing…*

Most of these 'conversations' were carried on in rudimentary Portuguese and sign language. Because our workers came over from the Brazilian back country, very

Damnedmudhut

few of them spoke English. It was up to us to learn to speak their language.

Don and I summoned Harry and the house-builders together one day after they had put the corrugated roof on our house.

"Harry, please impress upon the men that the most important thing now is to get this house finished! Ask them please not to dawdle over little things that can be taken care of after we move in. Let's just get it painted, inside and out, so that Jan and I and the baby can move up here." Harry translated all that into Brazilian Portuguese. The men nodded agreeably.

The following day Don and I flew up to deliver another load of our belongings and some supplies for the pantry. There we discovered the 'master carpenter' dreamily carving scallops over the guest bedroom door. He'd already finished doing ours. So much for our instructions of the day before. Besides, I hated the look of the scallops. For three years.

With no dressers, chests, or any shelves of any kind yet built, our belongings were piled in the center of each room. Don stored some of the mining equipment in the house too, for safekeeping. I particularly appreciated the decorative touch of a twenty-pound diving helmet just inside the front door.

"I can't *wait* for tomorrow!" I exclaimed to Don as we closed and locked the front door. We were headed back to Good Hope for our last night there. The following day we would be officially in residence at our new house, now painted a beautiful buttercup yellow instead of mud-color.

Next morning Don took the back seat out of the Grasshopper and managed to cram Diana's basket/bed in along with most of our remaining clothes. He would make one flight to drop those things off at Marquis, then come back for the two of us. Meanwhile, I'd give our cherub her final 'Good Hope bath' and get her ready for the flight 'home.'

This routine was a wearying one. Our bedroom was in the corner of the house farthest from the kitchen, my source of warm water—on the wood stove. The bathhouse was almost as far from both kitchen and bedroom. So bath time was also exercise time for me. But the routine went smoothly. "Diney" kicked merrily on the bed while I grabbed towel and baby shampoo and headed for the kitchen. It was a quick run with the water kettle to the bathhouse where I filled the basin and readied the shelf with soap and towel. I noticed Neka and Pauline, ever-present baby on her hip, watching me as they usually did. They were fascinated by this running/bath routine and never missed a day of watching. Now, back to the house to grab the baby before the water got cold…

On the way back to the bathhouse I met Neka, Pauline and the baby –now noticeably a few shades lighter, wrapped in— *my baby's towel*, noticeably a few shades darker! The basin, when I reached it was, not surprisingly, half full of muddy brown water. I turned to yell at Neka and Pauline at this final outrage, but of course they were nowhere to be seen.

I'd have begun the whole routine over again, but the distant hum of a plane engine meant Don would be back and ready to load in a few minutes. A quick sponge bath would have to do Diney until we got to our own house where, I hoped, there'd be water. *I won't be sorry to leave those two whiz kids behind!*

8
Marquis Living

"Have you radioed BG Airways to make sure they'll do the flight as we asked?"

"Yep," Don answered, "it's all set. Our airstrip's in top form. Harry and I walked it yesterday and inspected every foot of it. It's as good as it will ever be; hard as a rock. Glad we haven't had any recent rain." He hesitated. "You know, I wouldn't have anybody but Julian fly a DC-3 into our valley. It's gonna take all his skill to maneuver that baby in *and* out. But he's the best pilot I've known, yet."

Don was talking about our new friend, Julian Pieniazek, head pilot for BG Airways. We both liked and admired Julian, a tall good- looking Polish fellow with a ready smile and unending sense of humor. He and his wife, Freda, lived at Atkinson Field, so we had run into them many times. It was Julian who flew me to Georgetown before Diana was born and who flew us both back to Good Hope. He was a "regular" at the Gorinsky's table, especially on alternate Fridays when he brought them mail and supplies.

Early next morning Don left Marquis and flew off to Good Hope to meet the DC-3 there. It was fully loaded with our mining equipment and supplies, and Julian wanted Don on the plane to guide him every minute of the approach to

Marquis, where I was waiting. My heart leaped into my mouth at the first sound of the DC-3. I ran to the edge of the airstrip to watch Julian's approach. There was no room for error on this landing. Coming down the narrow river valley, Julian deftly maneuvered the huge plane between the mountains. I held my breath as it settled lower, then lower. He put it down "on a dime" at the far end. My sigh of relief was audible as I watched him turn around and taxi back to where I stood to at mid-airstrip, where our crew was waiting to help unload. I reached the plane just as Julian climbed down the ladder.

"Jesus!" he exclaimed, running his hand over his head as if to erase a troubling thought. He squinted at the low mountains ringing our valley. "How'm I gonna get *out* of here?"

Don grinned from ear to ear as he climbed down the ladder. Vicky Fikes, Julian's co-pilot, was shaky as he emerged. The color slowly came back to his face as he gratefully placed both feet on the ground.

I'll ride with you on the way out, too," Don offered, giving Julian a clap on the back. I know every bank and turn to be made. You'll have no problem, Julian. Besides, the plane'll be empty!"

The four of us made our way up the path to the house, leaving the crew to unload, under Harry's supervision, machinery and supplies. In spite of the hot sun, our house with its smooth cement floor and thick adobe walls offered shade and a measure of cool. I apologized for the "lunch."

"You'll have to come back after we have the 'fridge' working," I said, offering them a seat on an army cot that served temporarily as our sofa in the living room. Our house needed several pieces of furniture, including a dining room table and some chairs. We had one canvas chair and two high stools the crew had cobbled together. So the four of us sat at different levels as we munched on my offering of canned corned beef and crackers. "I'll never get up to Nellie's standards, but next time I promise you'll get better fare."

"Never mind, Jan," Julian smiled. "It's good to see you and the baby in this perfect little valley paradise. I'll be glad to fly in supplies any time, but I don't think BG Airways will let me bring the DC-3 in *here* again! Freda sends her regards. She sent this little gift for Diana," he said, offering me a soft tissue-wrapped package.

I opened it immediately. "Oh Julian! It's darling. And I'll bet she crocheted it herself! He nodded and smiled as I admired the sweet little bonnet Freda made. I was mindful that Julian and Freda, married several years, had not had a child, something they dearly longed for. "I'll write her a note to take back with you. Please don't tell her about the meager lunch I offered you."

Don tied a couple of hammocks in the "guest room" for Vicky and Julian so they could rest while the men finished unloading the plane. After I'd written the note to Freda, we too took advantage of the break to take a nap while our baby slept on her army cot. At least Don and I had a bed in the house. But it would be slow going to furnish the other rooms. The mining operation took precedence over tables and chairs.

"See you in a little bit," Don called back over his shoulder as he and the two pilots started off down the path to our airstrip an hour later. "I know Vicky isn't looking forward to this take-off, but we'll be fine with Julian at the controls. Don't worry. I'll be back for dinner, if not sooner."

As I watched the take-off from our small strip, I knew everything would be fine. No one could fly like Julian and Don was on board, crouched between the two pilots, directing Julian's every move, the pressure of Julian's feet on the pedals. As I'd seen the Grasshopper do so many times , the DC-3 took off just before the end of the airstrip. Immediately banking right while still climbing, and then left to avoid the small mountain on the opposite edge of the river, the lumbering plane gained altitude. I watched it as long as I could and then turned back to the house with its piles of wood shavings and clay dust. If my kerosene stove and Diney cooperated, I might have some fresh bread ready for dinner.

At least the kitchen was usable. At the back corner of the house, two half-walls were screened from counter level to the roof, offering a beautiful upriver view and a cross breeze. Don and I had put a lot of thought into the siting of the house and he had the foresight to plant papaya, orange, and lemon trees months before when the foundation was first laid out. The citrus took some time to establish themselves, but the papaya trees were growing like weeds. In the kitchen, stained and varnished hardwood counters ran along the outer two walls. A small pantry *had* held a small supply of canned hams, juices, and vegetables, but the crew made short work of those on a particularly taxing day before we moved in. After all, the supplies were *there,* the doors were not locked, and no one had said *not* to take them. Harry set the crew straight shortly after we discovered this transgression.

What we hadn't counted on was the fact that we were now not only the "new kids on the block," but also the *strange* new kids on the block. We were **entertainment**! Xavier, our "master carpenter" had convinced his entire family to move to our compound where our daily lives provided scenes better than a drive-in theatre. While Xavier worked on the dredge with the other crew members, his wife and stair-step children stood, noses pressed to the screens, watching my every move. They were ever present.

Other "neighbors," sometimes as many as fifteen, hiked the distance to our little green valley from their own villages to look in on us. Literally. During that first month, several pairs of dark brown eyes followed the bright plastic measuring cup in my hand from counter to bowl and back to counter again. They watched as I changed Diney's diaper. If I had her in her own room where the windows were well above eye-level as they were in our bedroom, they climbed on discarded crates, large rocks or each other's shoulders in order to get a better view. Timing was everything when we wanted to visit the throne room.

Rarely did the expressions on the brown faces change. They watched quite somberly the mixing of bread dough, the lighting of the oven. Once in a while something would tickle them and they would giggle interminably. I always wondered what it was in my routine that amused them so.

My pigeon Portuguese did me no good the day they discovered how the doorknob worked and let themselves in for a tour of the house, with Mama Xavier nursing the smallest, and eight little ones in various stages of dirt and undress following. I frowned and pointed the way to the front door, locking it behind them.

This went on for a month before I lost all patience with being the center of Macusi and Brazilian attention. I'd wakened early one morning and sleepily found my way to the bathroom sink to splash some water on my face. Grabbing a towel from the nearby rod, I extracted my face from it to find an Indian face eight inches from mine, on the other side of the screened window. That face grinned as I jumped.

Xavier's tribe was in place early to watch as I placed the colorful Melmac dishes on the counter and drew the stools up to it so Don and I could have breakfast.

"All I want is a little privacy," I grumbled to Don,

whenever we ate at the counter. But he had mining concerns on his mind and barely noticed the brown faces and eyes not two feet from his. Later that day, I sought out the one corner of Diney's room, which couldn't be seen from *anywhere* outside the house. Trying to regain a sense of perspective and humor, I sat on the cool cement floor and leaned against the yellow wall. The smell of burning bread brought me charging back into the arena. That did it.

"Maxim! Maxim!" Grabbing a pot holder and pulling the pans from the oven, I called to one of our workers, "Come! Run!"

"Yes, Mistress," Maxim panted as he reached the house.

"Maxim, you must tell these people they cannot stand outside the house all day watching me," I told him, pointing at the little tribe waiting for the next event. "Please tell them politely, but tell them firmly *to go home*!

"Yes, mistress," Maxiim grinned as he turned to translate my message into the Macusi tongue. He turned back to me. "They are going, mistress. They say, 'thank you,' mistress."

In spite of myself, I smiled. They'd meant no harm and even though they'd been ordered away rudely, it had not hurt their feelings. I went back to the kitchen and sliced off the blackened tops and bottoms of the bread and coffeecake.

Don flew back in time for "tea" later that day. He had flown to Good Hope to see if BG Airways was going to allow another DC-3 flight in to our strip. As we sipped our tea and "tucked into" the coffeecake, we slapped at the small black specks on our hands, arms and necks. The cabourri flies were still plaguing us, even in the screened house. The tiny blood-sucking flies were easily able to crawl through the mesh.

"I think I've got the solution," Don boasted as we

discussed this problem for the umpteenth time since before moving in. "I'm going to 'paint' oil on the screens so that the cabourris are soaked with it as they crawl through. They won't be able to fly and they'll die!" The very thought of oil-soaked cabourris gave us a huge sense of joy.

Don's solution worked. The screens, clogged with disabled cabourris and dust, cut down a bit on the gentle breezes that wafted down the valley, but regular cleaning with a stiff brush and re-oiling became routine, and we were even able to pack away the netting that had covered Diney's cot day and night. I stowed my long pants and long-sleeved shirts, donned shorts and sleeveless tops, and felt many degrees cooler.

Since mining matters took precedence over personal comfort, it took us until October to get in good shape, house-wise. The outside of the house was painted a pale yellow, the inside rooms were cool, pastel colors. Bookshelves and shelves for clothing were in place, and I had started marigold and zinnia seeds in flowerbeds next to the house. We were ready to receive *invited* guests.

"Shall I write to Ray and tell him we now have running water *in* the house as well as next to it?" Don was referring to our friend, Ray Helminiak, from Wisconsin, who'd been angling for an invitation to come down to visit. He was one of the company stockholders as well as a dear friend. "Since it's mail plane day tomorrow, I think I'll send him an invite to come on down with Marilyn. "

Ray's answer was as immediate as it gets in the interior of B.G. "I'll be down within two weeks," he wrote. "I want to decide for myself whether or not this whole thing is a big hoax, Don," he wrote jokingly. "Unfortunately, Marilyn can't join me. She's expecting our son and heir!"

Ray arrived with a duffel bag full of Dial soap, Gerber's Junior Baby Food, food coloring that came in familiar tiny bottles instead of the three pound packages I had to order from Bookers in Georgetown, and a suitcase full of other food goodies. Undoubtedly Ray had thought we'd serve him nothing but casava root and snake meat during his stay.

An adventurer at heart, Ray, enjoyed every minute of our *exciting, different, romantic* lives. "I am in a constant state of amazement!" he exclaimed, time and time again. "Indians, snakes, jungle, lack of communication, small plane, hammocks, hunting! Wow! This is really exciting!" Of course he was leaving after ten days. Which he did, but not before telling us that as a stockholder, he was most impressed with our undivided devotion to the company.

For our part, Ray's visit provided ten days of intelligent conversation with another white person from the 'States. We were also grateful that the other stockholders would receive a first-hand report of the mining operations without Don having to fly up to give it to them.

Our "damned-mud-hut" became more and more livable. I brought in the pretty orchid plants Harry had found to hang from the rough beams across the living room. In fact, Diney's first word was not "ma-ma" or "da-da". It was "p-tee" as she pointed to the nearest orchid.

Not long after Ray's visit, we finally gained a dining room table. We felt quite grand, indeed, seated alongside the glossy reddish brown surface, eating in style instead of on packing boxes and stools at the kitchen counter. Life was good. Before dinner Don and I would fix a drink, lean against the counters, gleaming in the late afternoon sun and look out at the panoramic view of Brazilian mountains across the river. In the rainy season we would catch glimpses between our fruit trees of the sparkling, swift moving Ireng River. No longer were the Indians staring in, so we could dally and stare out.

More small orchards dotted our compound. Lemon, orange, and grapefruit trees were within view of the kitchen. Farther out were the mangoes, guavas, papayas, avocados, bananas, pineapples, and lime trees.

Through trading we collected a couple dozen chickens. In fact, when Ray was visiting the hens were laying up to a dozen eggs a day, which certainly helped the menu. I thought that would last forever, but there were weeks when I hoarded two, then three eggs –and was faced with the dilemma of making a cake or scrambling them for breakfast.

The morning I realized Marquis valley had been discovered by the cushi ants was a bad one. We first met up with these "parasol ants" as the native Guyanese called them, at Good Hope.

"Don! Come quick!" I wailed from the kitchen early one morning. "Our trees! Our poor little lemon trees!" Don came running and the two of us were out the back door like a shot, in time to watch the "caboose" of the long train of ants move off toward the river. Overnight, they had stripped our lemon trees of their leaves.

We'd already spent a bad night with the resident grey foxes yelping under our bedroom window. Then, having wakened us, they headed for the chicken coop and caused such a ruckus there that Don leaped out of bed and grabbed his shotgun to quell that rampage. Such was our life in the peaceful valley of Marquis.

But there was *good* news! At long last the beautiful baby crib Mother and Dad shipped from Michigan arrived in Georgetown. It took only three days to go those thousands of miles. Unfortunately it sat in Her Majesty's Customs for eight weeks. Our agent in Georgetown was doing his best, he assured us, but our beautiful daughter had now learned how to turn over on her army cot and several times landed on the unforgiving cement floor.

"I've radioed Anthony to send the crib on *any* plane to the interior," Don said one morning after signing off from his ham radio. It means I'll have to meet the Orinduik, Lethem, Good Hope, Kamarang, and Karanambo planes on Tuesdays and Fridays. Lord, we could have built six cribs for her by this time!" After a couple of weeks of flying back and forth across the savannahs, the crib was consigned to Good Hope and actually arrived there. Now, we needed to get it to Marquis.

The crib was too unwieldy for our small plane. It would have to be transported upriver by boat. Harry volunteered. The Ireng was low this time of year and the trip would be hair-raising. Four days after he left, we heard the welcome sound of a boat motor.

"Here he comes!" I called excitedly to Don who joined me in a race to the river's edge where we could grab the crated crib, lest it fall overboard in a fitting climax to our long tale of woe. I'm sure Don expected a celebratory lunch once we got the crate up the slippery bank and dragged to the house.

"Lunch can wait until we set up the crib," I announced firmly. I sat on the cool cement floor feeding Diney, watching with joy as Don and Harry assembled the most beautiful baby bed in the world. As I wrote Mother and Dad later that afternoon: I am so happy! God's in His heaven and all's right with the world.

I have never used that phrase since without a feeling of dread consuming me.

The Wild Ireng River

9

Grasshopper Farewell

Twenty-four hours after making the happy proclamation to my family that "all's right with the world," our first tragedy hit.

"I'll be making several trips today, Hon," Don said that Monday morning as he started out of the house. "I want to bring two divers up from Good Hope and Caesar needs to catch the Orinduik plane to Georgetown tomorrow. I'll refuel between trips and bring him here for dinner and the night."

That was something to look forward to. We didn't get much company, news or occasion for intelligent conversation. So I looked forward to having Caesar as a guest, if only for a meal and the night. Don and I needed a diversion and this one came with a great sense of humor and all current savannah gossip.

Don made the first trip quickly. The divers must have been waiting at Good Hope's airstrip and helped Don with the refueling. I glanced out the front window and saw the two divers carrying their gear and walking through the tall grass toward the barracoun. Don taxied the "Grasshopper" back to the beginning of the airstrip, turned, and revved the engine. Always cautious, he would be checking the systems again before take-off. I turned back to the kitchen, already thinking of what I'd fix for a special dinner.

I heard the roar of full throttle, the gradual dwindling of sound after the plane passed the house going full speed toward take-off. And then suddenly—silence. My heart froze in the awesome stillness of the afternoon. Nothing. Not a sound. I ran to the dining room window to search the end of the airstrip. Our Grasshopper, a glider now, was making a slow, noiseless turn away from the river, just over the treetops. Our flight instructor's voice immediately sounded in my head. *Don't ever try to make it back to the airstrip!* But there was no choice.

I snatched Diney from the living room floor and ran with her out the front door, my feet scarcely touching the path to the airstrip. I could see our plane disappearing below the treetops.

"Oh, God. Please, God!" I gasped, my mouth dry with fright. I was afraid to look, yet grim fascination kept my eyes glued to the spot where I'd last seen the Grasshopper. My heart was pounding as I ran, my panting the only sound in the heavy afternoon air.

"Chaga," I gasped, thrusting Diney at him. "Take the baby!" I could run faster now and kept listening for the sound of an explosion. But there was none. I kept running until I was almost at the end of the airstrip. My eyes were still glued to the spot where I'd seen the plane go down.

Then, suddenly, he was there—walking out of the bush. And all in one piece. I stopped dead in my tracks. Sheer joy held the enormity of what had just happened at bay.

"Well, that's that," Don understated a few minutes later when he reached me. "I made the clearing and just made it between the two rocks. But there was another one hidden in the grass and it got the landing gear. The plane nosed over and drove the prop into the ground. The left wing is almost off." I got the picture.

Except for a few nicks from flying glass, Don was completely unharmed. But he looked dreadful. I could sense the plane was a total loss. We were hundreds of miles from civilization, so there wasn't much hope of salvage or repair.

Don and I put our arms around each other and silently walked back up the strip to retrieve our now wailing child from Chaga's arms. It was hard to absorb all that this meant, immediately and for the future. As the initial shock wore off, we alternated between feeling helpless and feeling sad. Our little green Grasshopper surely deserved a period of mourning. It had carried us happily and safely wherever we wanted to go for over a year.

That night, over dinner, we settled down to serious thinking about the mess we were in. Our only contact now with the outside world was our ham radio. Our only transportation by boat down the Ireng River, a day's trip and a dangerous one.

Word of Don's accident spread quickly, by radio and by the ever-efficient "bush telegraph," a strange sort of extrasensory perception that carries information through the bush and over the savannahs. Don radioed Atkinson Field to report the crash, telling them no one had been injured. Atkinson in turn radioed an American pilot, Art Ferriman, flying for the Pilgrims' Holiness Mission in the Pakaraima Mountains north of us. Ferriman immediately flew next morning to Good Hope to pick up Caesar. The pair flew to Marquis. Joe Tesarek, another small plane pilot in B.G., flew in that day too, bringing food and the new foreman who had been waiting with Caesar.

Suggestions for our wellbeing flew from all directions. Caesar and Nellie wanted Diana and me to stay with them

Grasshopper's Final Landing

at Good Hope. Mother and Dad, when they got wind of it, wanted me to come "home." Don and I mulled over the dangers of remaining at Marquis and carefully considered the alternatives.

I made up my mind. "I'll be better off here with Diana in familiar surroundings. I don't see how you can possibly cook, keep house *and* work ten hours a day on the barge. I'd be sick with worry and there'd be no way for you to get a message to me. No, I'm staying."

I couldn't tell if Don was relieved or ready to argue the point. But he saw my determination and knew well enough not to disagree. The last thing we needed now was a quarrel.

"Maybe you're right," he said, folding his arms around me in a protective hug. "And since you're so determined, let's start thinking of the problems that face us and how we're going to deal with them. "We're planning a trip Stateside for Christmas and that's just over two months away."

"We'll be okay," I stated firmly, needing to convince myself of this truth. "We just need to be extra cautious about *everything* we do. We can't let anything happen to us, the men or the machinery now."

The considerations were many: food supply, kerosene to keep our appliances running and our Tilley lamps burning, gasoline for the mining equipment, rations for the men, our safety, and sending and receiving messages. Harry volunteered to make the boat trip once a week to Good Hope, so we needed to organize food, rations, and mail to coincide with that. Nellie and Caesar would wait anxiously for the sound of our boat motor when Harry would bring word to them that we were all still alive and kicking. They, in turn, would send back fresh fruit, garden produce, and much needed notes and news of the outside world. It was our turn, then, to wait anxiously for the sound of the boat motor announcing Harry's return.

In mid-November Harry brought us word that Don's brother, Bob, and a young pilot, Ernie Argentati, were flying down with a new plane for us. The Piper Tri-Pacer should arrive any day now. Our permanently furrowed brows began to relax and I planned a celebratory dinner—more lavish than we'd had for weeks— for the arrival.

Three afternoons later the sound of an unfamiliar plane engine droned into earshot. "There she is!" Don shouted enthusiastically, running out the front door. He stood in front of the house, squinting into the sun. I picked up Diney, joined Don and the three of us headed down the path to our airstrip. We watched the little plane, bright and new, settle onto the dry packed soil that was Marquis landing strip. Our plane. A four seater. It would become our pride and joy for the remaining years in South America.

"Three six Delta," Don read on the plane's tail. "Sounds good to me."

The Tri-Pacer took a while to unpack. Bob and Ernie had stopped at some of the islands along the way and filled the plane with bottles of wine, island sweet treats, *and* canned hams. These were squeezed in beside the Christmas presents Don's family had sent along just in case we didn't make it "home" for Christmas, as we still hoped to do.

 We had a merry feast that evening . Ernie was a happy-go-lucky, fun kind of guy, but a serious pilot. A twinkle never left his eye as he told the tales of the flight down from Milwaukee. We both instantly liked and admired him.

We'd pumped up the Tilley lamp several times that night before finally tying the two hammocks in the guest room in the wee hours of that exciting day. It had only been seven weeks of isolation for us, but seemed much longer.

Don and Ernie were out early the next morning, taking

our new plane through its paces. Also a single engine, also green like our Grasshopper, Three-Six Delta, was a four-seater. Being in command of a plane once again and learning its characteristics, changed Don's whole personality. It was as if he'd been let out of jail. He was now free to carry on where he'd left off.

Ernie also took the time to teach Don instrument flying. Up 'til then we'd followed only VFR (Visual Flight Rules) and Don ate up the learning like a hungry man. He knew well enough the situations to avoid but also knew the day would come when avoidance wouldn't be an option. Weather could be the enemy. Fronts could move in or clouds could obscure not only the ground but uncharted mountains as well.

Bob and Ernie stayed with us a week. Once again mobile, Don and I realized how wearying and worrying our situation had been over those weeks. By comparison, we now felt utter freedom. Added to that was good company and lively conversation. Life was good again.

After Bob and Ernie left, the weeks remaining until Christmas holidays flew by, crammed with preparations to leave Marquis for a month. Don worked endlessly on the barges, trying to decide if their present locations were productive enough to warrant leaving them there during our absence. Or, should our new foreman, Nelson, move all the equipment upstream a couple of miles? On those barges, custom built by our men, sat our entire investment in the mining company. Heavy equipment for dredging, pumping, sorting gravel, diving helmets and hoses, —it was all there floating on the Ireng River, tied expertly to the riverbanks to allow for the change in water level as the rains came and went.

Don finally decided to let Nelson move the barges while we were away.

Don and Tri Pacer

"It makes sense, Jan," he told me at the end of one particularly unproductive day of pumping gravel, looking for diamonds or, at very least, indicators. "While I'm wrestling with never ending questions and suggestions from stockholders and convening board meetings, Nelson can dismantle the barges and machinery and move it all to a new location."

That decided, we concentrated on packing and planning all that we needed to accomplish during our "vacation."

Everyone in the compound, workers and their families, wanted us to bring something back for them from the 'States. Most requests were reasonable, but Don drew the line when one of the divers said he wanted an accordion!

We crammed an empty duffle bag in a suitcase, along with hundreds of diapers and a beautiful blue nylon snowsuit for Diney. On our return to B.G . we would look like Santa.

The three of us flew the Tri-Pacer to Ogle Strip, a small airfield on a sugar estate east of Georgetown. Someone could easily watch over it there because Ogle was closer to Georgetown than Atkinson was. PanAm flew us to Idlewild where, surprise, it was not 102 degrees. Diney was fine, snuggled in her snowsuit as we descended the steps onto the tarmac. (This was in the days, of course, before enclosed ramps provided a measure of comfort to passengers.) But PanAm attendants thoughtfully wrapped Don and me in blankets for our short jog to the terminal.

It was my tall, serious, Lincolnesque Uncle Mitchell who met us in the terminal. At the sight of us his jaw dropped, his eyes closed, and a pained expression crept over his face. Not only were we wrapped in blankets, but we were also carrying Wai Wai Indian bows and arrows.

"Hi, Uncle Mit," I called shedding my blanket as I ran toward him. "We forgot our coats in Georgetown...and aren't these great souvenirs?" I was addressing the crowd of startled onlookers as much as my uncle. They accepted the loud explanation better than he did.

"Your Aunt Mildred sent this for you," he said, unsmilingly, thrusting a warm coat at me. Still recovering, he watched as I gratefully covered my pastel cotton dress with my aunt's heavy coat. By now Don had already returned his blanket to PanAmerican personnel so we looked more normal, much to my uncle's relief. He no longer looked like he wished to disown us all.

A few days in New Canaan, staying at my grandparents' house, afforded us the chance to buy some warm clothes for the weeks we would be in snowy Michigan and Wisconsin. Then, with "Merry Christmas" all around, we headed toward anxious grandparents in the Midwest.

Actually, we had two Christmases that year. One in Milwaukee with Don's parents, where our and their pleasure was quickly followed by business with the stockholders. On the 28th, we flew to Birmingham and celebrated a second holiday and New Year's Eve with my parents.

"This kind of makes up for last New Year's Eve when we were so far away," I said in response to my father's invitation to dinner and dancing. My sister, Bunny and her husband, Perry Morgan had flown in from North Caroina to join us so it would be a grand night for celebrating. "Nana" was only too glad to stay at home with her precious granddaughter and waved all of us, dressed in our finery, out the front door. But exhaustion set in for all of us and we were home by 1:00 a.m. Don and I were well fed and happy to be lying on a mattress instead of in a hammock.

What was to have been three weeks of business and pleasure combined, turned into six weeks of mostly business. Meetings with stockholders and directors of the mining company shuffled us from parents' home to parents' home, so that by end of January both mothers and fathers surely were of a mind that our return to South America was not such a bad idea after all. Until I announced to Mother and Dad that we were expecting another baby mid-summer.

I thought we'd have to rent a car to get to the airport, so reluctant were my parents to be any part of our return to "thatdamnedmudhut." Now not only were daughter and husband headed for sure disaster, but one and a half grandchildren as well! It's tough being a maverick. Tougher still, the parents of one.

Don had two days of business in New York City, which we reached from Willow Run (Dad did, after all, take us there) in the wee small hours of the morning.

"The only rooms available are at The Ambassador," Don announced on his return from the bank of pay phones. "Not exactly a family-type hotel, little tyke, so you'd better be on your best behavior," he warned nine-month- old Diana as he took her from my weary arms.

Best behavior it was. Dressed in beige linen with a long brown velvet sash, she looked nothing like a "bush baby" next morning as we sat down to breakfast amongst sedate groups of business men and wives. Our gray- haired waiter was overjoyed to lift Diana into a highchair (Surprise! They had one.) A hard roll kept her occupied as she and that waiter made fast friends; to the point where he surreptitiously brought out his wallet to show us pictures of *his* grandchild. We *ooohed* and *aaahed* appropriately, casting furtive glances in the direction of the maitre d' and hoping the warm and friendly waiter would not be reprimanded for warming the all-too-dignified atmosphere of the dining room.

The following evening, Don and I reluctantly gave our coats to Don's brother, Bob, who'd joined us in New York for those two days. The wintry January night was even more miserable in an unheated airport bus. Dressed once again in clothes suitable for South America, Don and I shivered until an Irish priest in the seat ahead of ours took pity on Our Lady of the Chattering Teeth and offered me the heavy sheepskin vest he'd been wearing under his topcoat. I took it gladly, smiling to myself at the thought that now we were leaving the 'States in much the same way as we'd come in weeks earlier—a sight to behold.

10

Good Housekeeping

Now there is just so much Bisquik you can fit in a suitcase. What had been an enormous load when I packed it was just a token supply unpacked in the kitchen at Marquis. Baking mixes were not a stock item in Guyana and I longed for anything that could enhance my culinary efforts as well as save time for other projects. Bisquik endeared itself to me with a recipe for a cake that didn't call for eggs—helpful when our chickens were on a laying strike. With careful planning I could make these four boxes last a few months. That is, if mice didn't discover them. Just looking at them on the pantry shelves made me feel inordinately wealthy.

Little by little I was adding items to our original menu of mostly corned beef or canned ham. There was plenty of that in the shop which Don had built next to the barracoun for his crew. I didn't mind raiding that supply in payback for the canned hams they'd lifted from our pantry months earlier. (They'd left a lone tin of corned beef on the top shelf after that raid. It must have been an omen.)

In those early days I could have written a cookbook titled 101 Ways to Serve Corned Beef , though I never found a way to combine it with peanut butter, the only other item in good supply both in Georgetown and in our pantry. Over time canned hams, canned butter, canned bacon and canned milk (Klim was the brand name some backward soul had devised) made their way onto our shelves while flour and sugar were in plentiful supply in Don's shop next to the barracoun just down the path from the house.

I fell into a routine of baking bread twice a week. The recipe in my cherished *Joy of Cooking* produced two loaves of bread, a pan of dinner rolls and a coffeecake (or cinnamon buns, Don's favorite.)

"That should last *forever,*" I'd sigh with relief at the end of a baking day. But it didn't. I'd slice the bread thinner and thinner, but it still disappeared all too rapidly. A couple of times when Don was on the radio to our agent in town, I tried ordering bread from Georgetown, coordinating the order to mesh with a Good Hope plane day. But by the time it completed its journey from Georgetown's bakery, through the furnace that was Atkinson Field's cargo terminal, to the interior, the bread resembled a little brown brick. (Had it been sliced, *Voila!* Melba Toast.)

Eventually, I came to enjoy baking day. To see the golden brown loaves and coffee cake cooling on the their racks in the afternoon sun, their crusts shining and slathered with butter and to smell the aroma of freshly baked bread as it wafted around the compound was a delight. Don could smell a freshly baked loaf from almost anywhere on the compound or river mining site. Nothing short of a diamond strike would keep him from "dropping by" to sample a crusty chunk while it was still hot. To think that such delicious morsels came from my mortal enemy, *The Stove.*

In our all-kerosene house, I cooked on a kerosene stove, got chilled drinks from a kerosene refrigerator, and read at night by a kerosene lamp. I ironed with a kerosene iron. I stored a jerrycan of kerosene in the pantry. I loved the

Macusi grating cassava

"fridge." The lamp was better than darkness. But I never came close to establishing a friendly relationship with either stove or iron. They were both "out to get me."

Each of the three burners had a corresponding knob indicating Off, Low, and High. *Relationships based on lies have no chance of success.* The burner was either Off or Way Too High. Mind you, it was necessary to turn the knob to High in order to let the wick soak in the kerosene for about a minute. "About" is the operative word. I had to sit on the floor, lift the burner base with one hand while lighting the wick with the other. Having three hands so as to have one to strike the match would have been helpful. If that burner had recently been turned off and was still hot, it would light like a bomb and singed eyebrows were a definite possibility.

Once the little circular ring of fire was going, there was nothing that could discourage it. Turning the knob to the ff in Off certainly didn't discourage it and it paid no attention when I got to the left side of the O. Once in a while I could turn it off, wait until a tiny lick of yellow flame danced around the circular wick, and then, QUICK! Turn the knob the right side of the O, just barely. Too far and it was flooded with kerosene and went out. Too late and I was looking at singed eyebrows again. Obviously I got the hang of it most of the time so as to produce those beautiful loaves. But it wasn't easy.

Nor was the kerosene iron. Like the lamps, it worked under pressure, with a continual hissing sound interrupted by an occasional "pop pop" causing palpitations of the heart to accompany the right arm exhausted by continually lifting the five pound iron. Here, too, were little wells to be filled with kerosene, a knobbed pump to create the proscribed amount of pressure, and a small hole in the side in which to pour the alcohol for lighting. Here, too, was the challenge of getting the right temperature, right pressure, all systems in the right alignment, risking the singed eyebrows again. Here, uniquely, was the possibility of flaming alcohol running down my arm. (Who says Don had all the adventure?)

A generator rescued us from blindness caused by reading by kerosene lamp. Darkness fell pretty much all year 'round at 6:30, giving us a few quiet hours after dinner to spend with a book or, with luck, a Time magazine only three or four weeks out of date. The generator held four hours' worth of fuel so if we wanted to stay up past ten-thirty, we'd have kerosene lamps ready for lighting when the generator began to sputter and die.

I offer the forgoing to friends who, knowing how isolated we were, ask "But what did you *do* with yourself all day?" Further, before we were hooked up to a water supply, we had to fill the commode by hand. So what with back and forth to the sink carrying a container, it would take at least ten minutes to "use the facilities!"

Once hooked up to a water supply, the commode needed a cesspit. Digging this was an adventure in the charge of Dutch, the old porkknocker we'd met at Good Hope shortly after we arrived in the Rupununi. Having knocked about BG for twenty years, Dutch sort of adopted us, or we him. The site for the pit having been chosen, Dutch commandeered several of the diving crew to dig.

There were the usual kibitzers, of course, Indians who looked on silently with no understanding of our purpose. After three days, one of them broke the silence.

"When you gwana put leetle house on top, Mr. Dutch?" he queried. Obviously he was a well-traveled Indian. "It gwana hav be *beeg* leetle house to fit toppa dat hole, no?" Later, he was beside himself as Dutch and the workman laid logs across the hole and covered them with a good layer of dirt.

Don took this opportunity to describe modern plumbing to the onlookers, taking them to the bathroom window and pointing out the toilet. They were not impressed. Looking at the toilet and then towards the enormous project just completed, they looked at each other and shrugged in disbelief.

"You shoulda stop when you get nice small hole, then put leetle house on top," muttered their spokesman as he shuffled off.

But a flushing toilet was a definite plus and added to that luxury was a break for me now and then when Pedro would bring his wife to camp for a few days.

"Poud lavar ropa?" I managed in my best, practiced Portuguese, hoping for a "Si!" from Maria. Which I got. I gathered the small mountains of wash I'd been putting off and gave them to Maria who readily headed for the river and a broad, flat rock. Late in the afternoon, she'd appear at the kitchen door with a monstrous bundle of clean, folded clothes and diapers then happily walk down the path to the shop where she could buy a few yards of cotton print for a new dress. Never mind the few items that floated downriver. Maria was a treasure.

One night after dinner as Don and I sat reading, Don looked up from his *Air Facts* magazine which had come with the mail on the Good Hope plane that day. "Where's your gun? Jan," he asked, out of the blue.

"In the library, I guess," I replied not looking up from my Good Housekeeping magazine.

"Used it lately?"

"No, haven't had to."

"Better check it over. Never know when you might need it."

"Um-hum." My reading interrupted, I remembered something that had occurred to me a few days earlier.

"Don?"

"Hm?"

"Where should I shoot him?""

"Who?"

"Anyone who tries anything."

"Depends."

"On what?"

"What's he up to?"

"Oh, I don't know, breaking in, acting menacing, something like that."

"At his feet." He paused. " If that doesn't scare him off then shoot to kill."

I don't think I can do that. Hopefully that'll never happen. Back to the second of a three part series in Good Housekeeping while Don continued to look longingly at advertisements for aviation gear. Just your typical husband and wife conversation.

As the generator sputtered, we put down our reading matter and got up to go to bed. "I certainly thought that by now Alan would have sent up the aluminum foil I ordered weeks ago," I mused, referring to our agent in town.

"I'll check next week at Lethem. Maybe Georgetown is out of it entirely," Don replied.

This was a typical situation. Weeks earlier I'd run out of aluminum foil and put it on the list for our agent to send along. Knowing how specific I needed to be, I pointed out that it was "for kitchen use." Weeks before that request, I'd asked him to send up a couple of water pitchers. What showed up were two ten-gallon water coolers. Actually, except for the expense, I was glad to have storage outside the refrigerator for a supply of drinking water. (Caesar and Nellie took the other one off my hands, telling me what I should have asked for were "lemonade mugs.")

But why it should take so long to send up the foil

was beyond me. Until Don came back from Lethem the following week sans foil.

"There weren't any small parcels consigned to us," Don reported when he flew back that afternoon. "Boy, did I have a time with the BG Airways shipping agent, though," he continued. He kept trying to foist off a couple of 400lb bails of sheeting on me that obviously should have been on someone else's manifest.

"What kind of sheeting," I asked, afraid to hear the answer. "Aluminum?"

"Yeah, but... Oh, no!"

We stared at each other in disbelief. *This takes the cake!*

"I can't WAIT to hear the explanation for this one," I said finally. Which I did when we radioed down to Alan the following week. He'd somehow thought we needed to roof the kitchen.

And so it went, getting nowhere and everywhere as we learned *English* English and to be precise about everything. I'd ordered three double bed sheets and gotten six singles. I'd asked for a "pancake turner" and learned, after weeks of correspondence, that what I wanted was a fish- slicer. Our pantry shelves groaned under the weight of things I supposedly had ordered but didn't. Three 3lb cans of food coloring, for instance. *(Does Alan think I'm starting up a bakery in the interior?)*

Our can opener was working overtime. In fact, we were already on our second one. "Let's get a garden going," I said to Don one day when he wasn't so beset with mining machinery problems. "I brought some seeds from Georgetown on my last trip down and I'm sure Nellie would give us some of her tomato seeds." (Even though Georgetown was north of us, we always said "down" to town because the city was four feet below sea level. Everything was "up" from there!)

"Good idea," Don agreed. "As soon as I can spare Maxim from the barge, I'll have him dig a plot in back of the kitchen."

It meant signing up for an ongoing war with cushi ants, but the tomatoes, radishes, watermelon and wildly growing corn were worth the effort and served nobly to enliven our meals. Of course the corn attracted capibara, a huge, wild sort of pig, actually, the world's largest rodent, but a shotgun fired out the kitchen door periodically kept them at bay some of the time. Besides, there was really enough for all of us.

So I fought with the insects and Capibara while Don battled the ever-changing mood of the Ireng River. The garden investment was small, but thousands of dollars worth of mining equipment rested firmly on two huge barges on a river which could rise twenty feet in a night and play havoc with our livelihood. Life in the bush could never be called dull or routine. We fell asleep at night wondering what new challenge would step forward the next day, hoping we would be up to it.

11

Dutch

A few weeks after we arrived at Good Hope the first time, Don and I were summoned by a shout from Caesar.

"Come and see a *real* pork-knocker," he hollered.

Curious, we both came at a run.

"This is Dutch!" Caesar said loudly, gesturing at the weather-beaten man dressed in tattered khakis and bent over a stout stick. Dutch looked at me and touched the drooping brim of his droopy hat shading his tanned wrinkled face.

"Goot ta know ya," he said, wringing Don's hand with his own bony brown one and dragging the ancient felt hat off with his other. "I heerdt ya were here."

Since he had no teeth, Dutch's cheeks sank in. But his closed-mouth grin, which reached from temple to temple, and his twinkling pale blue eyes made me realize he was probably *not* 102 years old. In fact, he was 57.

As the men exchanged bits of news, I glanced at Dutch's feet, or rather at the bits and pieces of his feet protruding from his tattered shoes. *This is, indeed, a real pork-knocker.* I could picture Dutch knocking about the interior, panning for gold and diamonds with only a piece of salt pork in his

Don, Caeser and Dutch at Good Hope

pocket to stave off starvation.

Nellie called us inside for tea, so we sat at the end of the big dining room table, shouting at each other. Dutch was nearly deaf. Which is probably why he felt more at ease doing all the talking. That afternoon began our long friendship with one of the most unforgettable characters Don and I ever met. His history came to us over the next few years through his hilarious and hair raising tales, some of them probably true.

John Schilder was born in the Netherlands, as his nickname implied. As I remember, he was the youngest child and only son of a good family. With older sisters and being the apple of his father's eye, this responsibility was more than Dutch could handle. So he left his family home to find adventure and his fortune in the great wild world

Once Dutch started talking, it was hard to stop him. We had to piece his life together through his wild tales, never knowing which came when or how he got from Canada, say, to the Spanish Foreign Legion. *The French Foreign Legion I've heard of...but Spanish?* His speech pattern was fixed, every tale punctuated with "oonderstandt ya know" and "unt eny damn ting else" in several places. If he stumbled on a word or name "unt dingus" was brought in to play. And since he couldn't hear well, there would be no sense in supplying the word he sought. We all caught our cue when he paused to insert his cackling "heh, heh, heh" and laughed with him. We all loved Dutch. He was a source of entertainment and a bright spirit.

Diney *adored* him. All children in the Rupununi adored him. And he returned the feeling. Dutch could not bear to see children unhappy, so of course he gave them anything they wanted. After twenty years in the bush, he wasn't spending as much time panning for diamonds as he had when he was younger. Before we arrived in the Rupununi,

Dutch dressed up

he stayed at Karanambo, a ranch owned by Tiny and Connie McTurk, situated southeast of Good Hope. It was always to Good Hope that Dutch came for Christmas, though, because that was where the "schildern" were. If there was anything Dutch loved more than telling stories and children, it was a good party. And Christmas at Good Hope, as I've described, was always a good party, with lots of "schildern."

At one birthday party in Lethem for a member of the Melville clan, Dutch actually did us all the honor of putting in his teeth. But that didn't last long. Because they were such a foreign object in his mouth, as the night wore on and the rum flowed, Dutch pulled them out and either set them down carelessly, or dropped them. There was ensuing bedlam when a resident dog picked them up in his mouth and ran, party-goers in pursuit. Dutch laughed the longest of us all.

He'd spent the last twenty years panning the rivers north of the savannah. He found some diamonds and a little gold, but never his fortune. Some of these he "gave away to the girls," he said, but I suspect most of his finds went right back into the river during Dutch's infrequent laundering sessions. He never kept his diamonds, as other pork-knockers did, in a "kitty" or "chibi." These are hollowed-out pieces of bone or horn or hollow quills with a bit of cork as a stopper. Dutch preferred to keep his diamonds tumbling about loose in his shirt pocket with the result that often they'd go back into the river on laundry day. But he laughed when he told us that story.

Dutch came to stay at Marquis shortly after we moved in our own house there. He felt he could be of some help to Don even if it was only to look after the "schickens." Sometimes he'd hang his hammock in the barracoun, but other nights we'd invite him to have a drink and dinner with us and he'd sleep in the spare room. This was called a spare room not only because it was unoccupied, but also because it had no furniture in it. Unless the cement floor was strewn with a layer of ripening avocados, it was completely empty.

After these dinners, Don and I would listen to Dutch's ramblings until either the generator ran out of gas or the pre-dinner rum took its toll on Dutch's stamina. We heard how he was shanghaied into the Spanish Foreign Legion, how he escaped into Egypt when his companion slit a guard's throat before towing Dutch, who didn't know how to swim, across the bay.

Another time, Dutch told us that, while doing a stint in the U.S. Navy, he and his shipmates had been called in as extras in a silent movie starring Mary Pickford. This was one of his favorite stories, even though, as he pointed out, he and his buddies were grossly underpaid. "Unterstandt, ya know, ve vere ta ones dat didt all ta vourk. Undt tose big stars hadt only a few lines ta say undt while dey stoodt still."

Dutch had a special bone to pick with President Hoover, because it was he who kicked Dutch out of the U.S. "Undt such a nice place too," he related. "I vasn't doing any damn ting to hurdt nobody." Indeed, he was simply making a number of Chinese happy by smuggling them and whiskey over the Canadian/U.S. border. Dutch failed to see anything wrong with this, especially since he was making such a good living at it.

But he was to have the last laugh on Hoover. "Unterstandt, ya know, all ta deportees vere loadedt aboardt a boat, unt dat night ta tamn ting stoppedt in ta Boston Harbor. So I yumped ship. Heh, heh, heh." Dutch failed to clarify how this was managed, since he still did not know how to swim. But the tale was too good to bring up such details so we kept listening.

"Undt so, I schanged my name to Yon Yohnson undt I

get to San Francisco. Dat vas vhere I get into your nafy undt get to be in pictures with Mary Pickford." And so it went until the generator sputtered.

Dutch didn't go out into the bush to pan for diamonds much after he came to live with us. But once in while he'd leave, and after a few days Don would land at some outpost where Dutch would be recuperating from one of his fainting spells. He'd insist that he was all right because he was taking his despised medicine, foul-smelling stuff that his sisters sent him from Holland. Dutch felt this dark and evil-looking brew was endowed with near magic powers.

Perhaps it was, for Dutch was so farsighted he couldn't see a gaping hole he was about to fall into. He was so deaf he couldn't hear a rattlesnake if it were coiled at the end of his hammock. But he kept showing up alive and happy to see everyone. On one of our trips back to the U.S. we bought Dutch a hearing aid. This was a greater boon to all of us who had tired of shouting than it was to Dutch.

He had no sense of direction, yet often offered to guide newcomers through the bush. He claimed to have guided two priests to an area inhabited by unfriendly Indians who promptly murdered the two priests with their spears as Dutch turned and fled, tripped over a rock and fell, knocking himself unconscious. "Ya, you laughff," he said. "But I tink I rather be a running cowardt dan a dead hero."

Don and I found it hard to believe this account, but Dutch assured us that both Brazilian and Guianese newspapers wrote up the story after finding the bodies of the two priests, and this is how his sisters back in Holland found out where he was. In fact, the ensuing correspondence between Dutch and his family put quite a burden on him. He hated writing letters but, dutifully, would pen a few lines twice a year to his sisters.

"For me it is nutting because it is mostly lying undt

any damn ting else, he sighed. "I tell dem I'm seeing da most beautiful sight of a deer and her fawn feeding yoost a few yards avay. Undt about my nice little house next to da mountain." This last was almost his undoing.

His sisters wrote back that they'd like wanted make the trip across the ocean to see this little Paradise where their long lost brother was living. This would be the trip of a lifetime. Only not in Dutch's. He solved this small vexation by writing that a fire had destroyed not only his house but the outbuildings on his little farm as well. "Zo, I tell 'em not to come out ta me, heh, heh, heh."

12

1957: Growing Pains

L ooking back on 1957...we'd rather not. The year brought only one bright spot in mid-summer, the birth of our son, Thomas Scott.

We returned to British Guiana after our stateside Christmas '56 visit, we stowed the blue nylon snowsuit and Bisquick and looked forward with both energy and optimism. Eager to tap the new mine site upriver from Marquis, Don was ecstatic when he found that Nelson, the new foreman, had accomplished the nearly impossible assignment of transporting machinery, men, and barges upriver without a mishap.

"Now we can really get going," Don announced enthusiastically a few days after our return home. "We're going to have to build a short airstrip up there at Tipuru to get in some men and supplies," he continued, "but that shouldn't take too long."

Along with flying in men and supplies, parts and equipment would, inevitably, need to be flown out for overhauling. Trips upstream by boat were out of the question; as was the overland route by narrow trail, which was almost impossible, not to mention way too time-consuming. The short airstrip, beginning just feet from the river's edge and ending five-hundred feet at the base of a small green mountain, would require Don to make his flights at dawn, before the slightest tail-wind could develop. He knew it was risky. It was also necessary. Work began at the river's edge.

A week after construction on the airstrip began, the men were happily looking forward to its completion when, in the last five yards, they discovered what they thought were two sizable rocks to be dug out.

"We tried digging them out," Don reported that evening, as he sat down on the camp chair and peeled off his socks. "But those were only the tops of some ' big mamas.' I'm radioing Georgetown tomorrow for drill bits."

The drill bits were sent with unaccustomed speed and we received them in record time: a week later. But they broke and had to be sent back to town, along with an order for tempered steel bits of the same size and some dynamite. The bits were sent, again with surprising promptness, still taking a week, but instead of dynamite, we got a stack of forms to be filled out. Who would purchase the dynamite? How would it be transported to B.G. Airways? Where would it be stored until flight time? Who was the pilot in charge of the flight to the Rupununi? (No passengers could be allowed on such a flight.) Who would receive the explosives and how would they be transported to Marquis? Who would do the actual blasting and what was his blasting permit number?

"I've got the forms all filled out," Don said with a sigh that night as we were getting ready for bed. "But I'll have to fly Harry to town to get a blasting permit for him."

Problem after problem, delay after delay. Frustrating challenges sought Don out like a swarm of cabourri flies. When at last a small shipment of dynamite was delivered to Marquis, after being carried upriver on the trail, it proved to be no good. While waiting for another shipment, the men devised another, crude method for disposing of the rocks. They built fires around and over both rocks and kept them hot for three days. Then, they threw cold water from the river on them. The rocks cracked in several places. By the time the second, viable dynamite was received, the rocks could finally be blasted into oblivion.

The airstrip was completed within three days after the last explosion. But could we expect stockholders or board members to understand *why* it would take six weeks from our return to BG before we could start-up the mining operation?

"We'll just keep going, Hon," Don said at the end of that rare, successful day. "We still have a couple of months before rainy season begins and the Tipuru site should either prove itself or not in that time." *Talk about dogged determination.*

I could offer little besides moral support; that, and a relatively happy home with a delightful little daughter, growing stronger and smarter by the day. And, perhaps, a son in the next few months. What I knew about blasting rocks and mining equipment was precious little, but at least my shoulder and ear were available.

Days stretched into weeks, and Don spent his nights in sleepless tossing and fidgeting. Well, that made two of us, as my increasing bulk made rolling over in bed a major and wakeful effort.

"You awake?" Don said softly in the middle of one restless night.

"Um-hmm," I answered. "What's the matter?"

"We need a different cutter head for the dredge pump." This was said with such resolve I knew he'd been pondering it for days, probably not wanting to tell me, not so much that I'd catch his state of dejection, but because it was an admission he didn't want to make.

"The pump is almost useless in the heavy clay we've run into," he continued. "I need a cutter head that'll help break it up."

This new information worked magically to awaken me fully. "So, what does a new cutter head entail?" I queried, not *really* wanting to know—at least not then.

"Well, I can design it...but I'll have to get Denver Mining Company to build and ship it to us."

"Have any idea what that'll cost?" I asked quietly, my mind going immediately to the bank account. We'd been running out of money from the moment we landed in the Rupununi. Stockholders were loathe, they said, to send "more" money when, in truth, it was not "more" that we expected. All Don was asking was for the *original* capital to be sent. We were now eighteen months into the mining and we were still asking for what we'd been promised. Thank heavens the flying could produce some income.

"No. All I know is we need it, and I'm going to design in." With that resolve, he fell asleep. I lay awake a while longer, until the sound of rain on the corrugated tin roof lulled me to sleep, too.

We awoke to a downpour. Since he wouldn't be able to fly to the mine site, Don settled at the long table/desk in our "library" to work on the new cutter head design. It rained all day. He worked at the desk all day. When the rain hadn't stopped by dinnertime, we realized the solution to our immediate mining problem had been made for us. It was the end of April and rainy season had begun. The Ireng was now swollen and raging from the rains. Instead of a possible source of diamonds, it was a formidable adversary, bringing to an end, we hoped, a frustrating and depressing five months.

Since our baby was due at the beginning of July, I had made plans to return to Michigan in early June with Diney.

Don and I worked toward that departure. Don secured the equipment and dredges at Tipuru while I got household matters in order and packed for our time away from Marquis. We would leave Dutch in charge of the house and compound. Of course some of the men working on the dredge would not come back when we resumed work. That couldn't be helped.

"I think when you and Diney take off for the 'States I'll fly over to Venezuela to see what Bob's up to," Don announced one day in mid-May. He was referring to his brother who was helping to set up a mining operation on La Paragua, a tributary of the Caroni. "There'll be some guys over there I can bounce my cutter head design off of and we'll pool our ideas and information. That way I'll be better prepared when I join you in the 'States, later." With a plan, he was happier, now.

Once again, we went our separate ways: I to Michigan to await our second child's appearance and Don to Venezuela get help in solving another mining challenge.

This time my trip was a little easier—and drier. I'd found waterproof pants that were "Made in USA"for babies. (This was in the era before disposable diapers.) Contrary to the British made, these new discoveries actually kept my lap dry all the way to San Juan. It was a long layover, but I enlisted the aid of a dapper young student and a kindly gentleman to chase after fourteen month old Diana while I rested my bulky self on a bench.

"Bad news, I'm afraid, Jan," my father said as he greeted us at Idlewilde—now known as JFK Airport. "Grandma died day before yesterday, and we've just come from her funeral."

I was stunned. My grandmother, Dad's mother, was larger than life to me. She was an institution. I'd never considered that she could or would ever die. I'd spent so many happy summers with her and Grandpa in New Canaan, CT. Their big old white house, surrounded by pear and apple trees, two huge red barns, and an enormous vegetable garden, kept me well occupied when I wasn't reading on the huge screened porch. *Aren't those things supposed to last forever?* The house wasn't the same that night. But I was glad I'd given Grandma her first great-grandchild; sorry she would never see her second.

"Dr. Longyear says 'anytime now,'" I exclaimed gleefully to my sister, Bunny, who was waiting for this call in North Carolina. "Come on up so Diney can get used to her 'auntie." It was the end of June and the baby was due on July 2nd.

"Maybe he'll come on the Fourth and we'll celebrate with fireworks!" Bunny laughed when she arrived. It was a glorious summer in Michigan, Mother and Dad had their two daughters "home" in Birmingham, Michigan so pretty much all was well for the time-being. At least *I* was enjoying myself. The other three looked less and less satisfied as, morning after morning, I'd roll down to the breakfast table... with no sign of a labor pain in the immediate future.

On the fifteenth of July, Bunny, who was in the process of adopting a baby said "Sorry, Sis, but I can't wait any longer" and took off for North Carolina. –Just as Don arrived from Venezuela.

"I thought by this time, I'd find you with babe in arms," he grinned, trying to hug my bulk. "I had the airlines shove half a dozen passengers onto different flights, telling them I was in a race with the stork!" He was obviously in better spirits than when I'd seen him last.

"You could have *walked* and still have been in time," I groaned, now thoroughly dissatisfied with the delay. "But at least we can celebrate our anniversary tomorrow night and have dinner out."

As we talked over that candlelit dinner, devouring our lobsters, Don described his successful trip to Venezuela. "I've got my design for the new cutter head and everyone says it will work!" he said gleefully. "I'm sending the plans to Denver Mining tomorrow." *Such a romantic!*

"Tomorrow" became Thomas Scott's birthday at William Beaumont hospital in Royal Oak, Michigan. Not only was Don *not* handed his child right out of the delivery room, the new father had to peer at Tommy through the glassed in nursery containing, this time, mostly white babies. *Which one is mine?*

It was a tough time. Don was staying at my parents' house, but without me as a buffer. Mother and Dad hating that our daughter—and their granddaughter—were so far away, and knowing that things weren't going well with the company, wanted us to give the whole thing up.

"I'm not quitting," Don said decisively during his next visit to the hospital. "I'm flying over to Milwaukee tomorrow after I get you safely settled in with your mother and dad. If the mining company is to succeed, we have to get the cutter head not only ordered but paid for as well, so I've got some persuading to do with the stockholders."

My heart ached for him. *I* saw the whole picture, but realized that was hard for stockholders to do. Don had been working for sixteen months now without a salary, flying passengers and small cargo in his few spare hours to make money and pay the company debts. He would, I knew, work another sixteen months without pay to see the company succeed.

"Can't you convince them to recapitalize? I asked.

"Oh, they agree that's what we need. Trouble is, none of 'em have seen the operation first hand, and they all expected better results by now. So did we! Ray's the only one who's been down to see the operation, and he can't convince the whole bunch."

"You'll find a way. I know you will. We both know we can't go back without their support."

It would be a tough sell in Milwaukee. Don filled the stockholders in on challenges they could never have imagined: American-made equipment being used three thousand miles from repair and replacement; damaged O-rings that can't be replaced with differently threaded English ones; weeks of waiting between the ordering and the obtaining.

It was also a tough sell in Birmingham. Mother and Dad were certainly in agreement with the stockholders. So Don and I were at odds with the whole world. Neither of us could stand the thought of failure

Then, at the beginning of September, Don called from Milwaukee and the chipper sound of his voice told me there'd been a break-through.

"We're set to go," he shouted. Get Tommy's picture taken and his passport. I'll be over in a week to help you pack." And so he was.

"So they can make even a baby look terrible in a passport photo," he laughed when I showed him Tommy's.

We resumed 'Operation Duffel Bag" all over again: baby food, Bisquik, outdoor furniture for our indoors, two rugs to make our house more like home. The passport arrived and our day of departure was nearly at hand.

"It'll be so good to get back again," Don exclaimed, enthusiastically, on the eve of our departure for New York, then British Guiana. We were moving carefully around our upstairs bedroom, trying not to trip over suitcases, duffel bags, diaper bags lying all over the floor. "Mining will have to start right away. I don't want to lose another day!"

We'd planned our day of departure with great care,

trying to keep everyone happy, including a one-and-a-half year-old and an infant. Dad would, reluctantly, take us to the airport.

"Oh, I have to run down and get my vaccination certificate from Dad," I said, tripping over a suitcase. "I gave it to him for safekeeping."

But Dad didn't have it. "I'm sure I gave it to your mother," he offered. "Better ask her." But Mother didn't have it either.

We tore the house apart looking. Now *everyone* was upset, including both children. It was hard for me to tell whether Mother and Dad were upset because of the chaos or because, after all these weeks, they weren't going to be rid of us after all.

We missed the plane.

"No sense going as far as Puerto Rico and just sitting there," Don observed, correctly. "Let's feed the kids and get them in bed."

"Okay. But let's go out to eat," I replied. Mother and Dad don't even want dinner, but I'll drop if I don't eat something."

We said little over that dinner. We both realized a new vaccination, the reaction, then the results, would take more precious time than we wanted. *Can anything else go wrong?* I watched as Don pushed his food from one side of the plate to the other.

Mother greeted us next morning at the breakfast table, vaccination certificate in hand. "I can't understand how it got in *my* desk," she said sheepishly.

Don was on the phone to the airline in an instant and managed to make reservations for the following day.

The flight to New York relaxed the four of us. But the flight to San Juan was delayed by engine trouble. To which Diana and Tommy vehemently objected. Enough was enough and they wailed the next several hours away at Idlewilde.

In the wee hours of the following morning, Don herded his little flock aboard the flight "home." Aloft and settled, Don and I looked at each other and smiled across the two sleeping children between us. Don leaned his head back against the seat, closed his eyes, and reached for my hand. I saw his smile disappear and a visible question mark take its place. I shared the question. *Another year in South America... or the last?*

Diana at Marquis

13

For Services Rendered

The throng of servants I was promised—or at least imagined—never developed into a throng. At best, our help trickled in and out for a day or two at a time, well past our need. That first year, I coped with daily filling of the stove and fridge with kerosene. I filled the water coolers in the pantry every other day with a bucket filled from our overhead water tanks in the orchard. One of Don's crew took care of filling those from a pump in the river.

Bread had to be baked. When there was no beef, we had to catch fish or game or stew one of our old hens. (Nothing was so delicious then as chicken stew and dumplings using an old worn-out hen.) No part of a meal ever came from a frozen package and desserts and cookies were all made from "scratch." Our *Marquis cuisine* completely lacked add-water-and-stir type dinners and there was never anything in reserve in the freezer compartment of the fridge.

Don had become fairly fluent in Brazilian Portuguese because he dealt with the mining crew day after day. But while I understood much of any conversation, my own vocabulary of the country consisted of little more than, "Can you wash the clothes today?" And, "It is necessary to find the other sock." With helpers coming from the nearby

Macusi tribe, I'd resort to sign language unless Maxim happened to be around to interpret.

When we first moved from Good Hope to Marquis, I spent a good part of every day at a washboard in the kitchen sink. Eventually, I had case of Jergens lotion sent up by plane because my hands were, more often than not, raw and bleeding. No wonder I made a dash to enlist the aid of anyone who appeared in our valley.

In Brazilian:

"Your daughter wants to wash clothes?"

"Non."

"She doesn't want to wash clothes?"

"Si."

"**Will** your daughter wash clothes?"

"Si."

I was never so confused that *I* ended up with the bag of dirty laundry.

One thing was a given: when I *did* find someone else to do the washing, all the way from Maria, through Francesca, Rosina, and Naya, the clothes were certainly *clean*. A Brazilian or Indian woman, along with a good smooth rock in the river and endless determination, got them that way. The women much preferred to see a hole in the diaper or pair of trousers than a stain. Bleach was unavailable, except for the sun, so there were plenty of holes, but no stains. Much of the time, Diney's diapers were in tatters and Don's shirts and trousers were decorated with many mendings.

Maria came to us because her husband, Jose, worked for Don on the barge. That is, he moved slowly around the barge and consumed his share of rations. Maria was friendly and willing and it was she who taught me what little Brazilian I mastered. In the beginning, she spoke only Brazilian so I'd point and say the English word and she'd point and say the Brazilian equivalent.

Maria actually stayed a couple of months and looked headed for the category of permanent employee. *If Don can only put up with Jose a little longer.* But as she began to look obviously more and more pregnant, I developed a guilt complex as she hoisted a bucket of soaking diapers onto her head and start for the river.

"Don't worry, Hon," Don reassured me. "These Indians usually work right through their labor, anyway. She'll probably have her baby amongst my socks one day and come back up the bank with it tucked under her arm along with the clean clothes."

But Maria wanted to go home to have her baby and dirty clothes piled up again.

Francesca came next; and though her husband, Bebe, didn't know it, *she* was the only reason we hired *him*. Eventually Don and I decided Bebe took the prize as laziest fellow in all of South America. But his wife was a willing washer *and* ironer so was there any question of Bebe's continued employment? After giving many assignments to Bebe, Don decided his sole responsibility would be to pull the plane from the hangar before a flight and push it back in at the end of the day. This Bebe managed without feeling imposed upon.

A month or so into this happy relationship, Don gave Bebe a hoe and cutlass and asked him to clear a small plot for planting.

"I'd like to be ready when rainy season starts," Don said as they walked toward the area to be cleared. "By the way, Bebe, you know the eggs in the hen house are for the Patrua, (mistress of the house) so make sure Francesca knows not to take any." Though this was said in an off-hand manner, it was important. We'd gathered fewer and fewer eggs over the last month. I treasured each one a hen gave up just as

Don treasured every diamond he dredged up from the riverbed.

The following day after breakfast, I was rediapering Diney and putting her in for her morning nap when Francesca burst in the front door, clothespins and clothes line in hand. Shoving them at me without a word, she continued through the house and out the back door, slamming it behind her. She nearly collided with Don on the path.

I had started a smiling "Bon Dia!" but was left open mouthed.

"What was *that* all about?" I asked as Don came through the door.

"I'll see," he said, sprinting after Francesca.

I stood at the dining room window watching the two of them gesture and shout in the hot mid-morning sun. Francesca kept shaking her head violently and, finally, stomped off down the path.

"It seems we have offended her honor by asking her not to take eggs," Don explained when he came back in. "What I said to Bebe she took as an accusation and says now her pride won't allow her to stay."

"Can't we do anything to keep her?" I pleaded, eyeing the pile of clothes to be washed. It never seemed to get smaller.

"Nope. They're determined to go. But don't fall for that honor business. It isn't the real reason."

"You mean Bebe?"

"What else?" Don replied with a shrug. "It's no coincidence that he was supposed to start cutting a field today. Doing good honest work is too much for him." He headed for the library to find and settle Bebe's account.

Rosina came next. She was married to Domingo who worked for Don, too. Rosina had helped me out in a pinch when she visited Domingo at the mine site. She was twice as smart as Domingo and usually kept him in line, though Domingo fancied himself a prize for ladies. His roving eye gave Rosina jealous fits. Rosina and Domingo had terrible arguments day after day, after which Rosina would come up the path and announce, again, that she was leaving him. But she never did.

Domingo was slow and did have a roving eye, but he and Rosina made a good team when I planned a chicken dinner.

"I need a good old hen for stewing, Domingo," I'd tell him early in the morning, aware of his lethargy. "Bring it to me before '*tres horas.*'"

"Si, Patrua," he'd reply with a nod.

But Domingo and my chicken were never there at tres horas. I'd wait awhile and then go out to find Rosina. Fifteen minutes later the chicken was on the kitchen counter, plucked, cleaned, and ready for the pot.

Rosina and I had a good relationship. She had a pleasant, positive attitude. I'd awake in the morning to the swish- swish of a reed broom as she swept the cement kitchen floor. And while she coveted Diney's baby clothes, she never helped herself to them. Her day was complete when I offered an outfit now too small or a pair of tiny white sandals which never had fit my big-footed baby.

Don's help was somewhat steadier. When his foreman, Harry, got sick, Don found Nelson Doy and pried him away from his government job in Lethem. Harry was plagued by ulcers and eventually spent more time groaning in his hammock than out of it, so we gave him long leave. It was Nelson that Don was going to pick up on that fateful second trip to Good Hope when we lost the Grasshopper.

Although Nelson never found many diamonds for us, he worked harder and longer at it than any of the others.

Up at dawn, out on the barge fighting off cabourri flies he put his knowledge of machinery to good use. He handled the men as well as he handled the machinery, so that both worked efficiently even when Don wasn't standing over them. I appreciated him, though he gave me wide berth. I understood why.

When we first met, I invited him into the house to wait for Don. He spoke English beautifully. I offered him some cold lemonade and then excused myself, explaining that I had several chores awaiting me in the kitchen. Diney was crawling around the house, looking for her favorite fuzzy dog, "Morgan."

Apparently Nelson decided to sit on the couch and—without seeing it—on Morgan. Morgan "barked."

"Oh, Honey, you found Morgan!" I called, thinking I was addressing Diney.

Silence. Then the quiet opening and closing of the front door. I looked out to see Nelson walking quickly down the path. He wasn't the only one embarrassed.

Of course Dutch was around intermittently. We planned for him to come stay in the house each time we were away from Marquis for more than a few days. When that coincided with the worst of the rainy season, Dutch would eat his fill of watermelon, papaya and young ears of corn, *if* he could chase the marauding Capibaras from the cornfield. Another job would be to keep the house from washing away.

Don and I still had not fashioned canvas drops for our screened windows on the windward side of the house. If the wind blew the rain in, Dutch would have to move all the furniture to the inside wall, being careful to leave plenty of airflow around them so mildew wouldn't take over.

Several times when he came to stay, Dutch would bring with him an old Venezuelan crony, Don Pedro Miguel. He became a favorite of ours. This white-haired friend of

Dutch's was handsome, in a merry, wrinkled sort of way. Whatever he did, he did heartily and all of it during the 20 hours of his workday. I soon became accustomed to the sight of his cheery face outside the kitchen screen and the sound of his robust, "Bon dia, Senora!" in the very early morning. I had always been a morning grouch, but Don Pedro changed all that. Who could be grouchy in the face of such a greeting?

He could also bake the finest bread that side of the equator. He baked it in a mud oven fashioned from a huge old ant nest. No wonder Dutch loved him! No ant nest was safe anywhere very long after Don Pedro arrived on the scene,

Whenever any or all of us would fly off in our plane, Don Pedro always walked us to the plane and saw us aboard. "God carry you safely and God carry you back," he would say, as he closed the door of the plane. And He did.

Don had others on his revolving crew. There was Chaga—who thought my command of his Brazilian language a riot. Pedro Bandido, whose name meant bandit, was one. Don finally decided not to pay him his wages, but let him steal them, instead.

Maxim was a funny little round-faced Brazilian who had been at our compound from the very beginning. He was an invaluable asset because he spoke both Brazilian and the Macusi Indian tongue. His English needed polishing. Swear words were a major portion of his vocabulary, but I was deaf to them or found them amusing.

"Have you seen Mr. Haack, Maxim?"

"No, Mistress," Maxim would reply, sweeping his hat off his head and holding it politely with both hands in front of him. "I don't know where-the-hell-e-gone."

It was 'The Mad Peruvian' who bothered me.

"He's writing a book called *The Diary of a Paranoiac*,"

Don told me, days after this strange fellow wandered into our valley. He said he was willing to work for rations, so Don took him on. He wouldn't bunk with the other men in the barracoun though, preferring to make a "home" for himself in the wrecked fuselage of the Grasshopper out by the hangar. After the Mad Peruvian came on the scene, I made sure I knew where my gun was at all times.

Often Don wouldn't make it back before dark, and I'd be left alone in the house with Diney. Maxim was there, of course, down at the barracoun, and I could count on him to start up the generator as evening approached.

On one such night, after feeding Diney and putting her to bed, I decided to read for a while in the living room. Something made me get up and lock the kitchen door, something I rarely did. *I'm really getting paranoid since that guy arrived.* The front door was already locked. An hour into reading, I heard a small sound outside and let my eyes go to the front door. The doorknob was slowly, but definitely, turning. My heart leapt into my throat. As casually as I could, I got up from my chair, walked to the kitchen door to make sure it was locked and went into the bedroom where my pistol was kept. Making sure no one could see me from the outside, I undressed and got ready for bed—where I lay awake for the rest of the night, my gun beside the pillow.

I related this to Don the next day. He was furious. And probably scared, too. He confronted the Mad Peruvian, told him to leave the area, never to come back. A few shots at the defiant fellow's feet reinforced the order. The last we ever saw of him was as he walked out of our valley, followed by two of Don's men conscripted to make sure our Mad Peruvian went far enough to make it a long journey back, should he ever contemplate it. Weeks later Don heard our recently banished acquaintance tried grabbing a girl at a camp north of us. Two Indians heard screams and pulled him away, relieving him of a knife. They beat him, sent him across the river to Brazil, threatening his life if he ever came back to B.G. Last we heard, he'd gotten as far as Venezuela.

Rainy season was nearly upon us and I was getting "heavy with child." I coped as best I could with intermittent laundresses. But as the rains persisted through May and our departure for the 'States for our second child's birth drew closer, getting the clothes *dry* added to the problem.

"I'll ask Nellie if she knows of someone we can borrow for a couple of days before we leave," Don said as he left for a flight to Good Hope.

"Bring anyone," I called from the kitchen where a box of Tide and I teamed up once again.

But there was no one to be had at Good Hope, so Don flew on to Manari, a ranch near Lethem, where he "borrowed" a young girl who agreed to come help.

For three days Anna washed, morning and afternoon. And for three days it rained, morning, noon, and night. Socks and pants hung over the dining room table; diapers dried in the oven. Shirts draped from lines strung across the guestroom, and a cloud of steam rose above the ironing board as I tried to iron clothes dry.

Nothing could be left dirty or damp in the house while we were gone. Mildew would walk away with it. As it was, Diney and I arrived in Trinidad, New York, and Detroit smelling decidedly musty.

14

Ramdat

On the flight back to B.G. from the 'States, with our two children in September of '57, Don and I addressed the challenges that awaited us. One of them was permanent household help.

"I think we ought to hire someone from Georgetown and take him back with us," Don suggested, pulling Diney from the aisle as she was about to be mowed down by a beverage cart. "Then, even if he gets tired of working, he can't get out unless we take him," he grinned.

"Hmmm," I mused, pleased with this thought. "How about an East Indian house-boy with flashing dark eyes, pearly teeth, dressed in white tunic and trousers?" I joked in return.

It was with this image in my head that we arrived at Atkinson Field. And, with the exception of the "uniform," our wish was fulfilled with Ramdat.

A former hotel dining room waiter, Ramdat was keen on seeing the interior. He readily agreed to help me around the house and said he would help Don with whatever else needed doing once the household chores were finished.

He flew back with us to Marquis and settled in with surprising grace for someone who'd grown up in the loud and bustling city of Georgetown. When the dishes and sweeping were done, Ramdat would help gas the plane, fill the generator, feed the chickens, and gather the eggs. Eventually he not only set the table, served the meals, and cleaned up after but also would cook up our favorite dish of curried chicken and roti (Indian flat bread) when asked. With his mop of wavy black hair and a smile full of teeth, Ramdat was a willing worker. His flashing dark eyes were a bonus.

"This is the life," I remarked to Don one night after dinner. We relaxed in our camp chairs as the table was cleared and the dishes clinked merrily in hands other than mine. "I'm a true lady of leisure."

"You deserve to be after all this time," Don smiled. "We've run the gamut of hired help, haven't we? Thank heaven Ramdat seems content to be here."

Ramdat had been with us for two weeks when Don was unexpectedly called into town, and I decided to take the children and go with him. That left "Dot-Dot"—as Diney called him—in charge of the house. Dutch had left to visit the McTurks at Karanambo for a few days.

"This is a big responsibility for you, Ramdat," Don explained as we got ready got ready to leave. We tried to prepare him for every situation likely to arise in our absence, but Ramdat seemed fully confident and up to the task of custodian. "Let's see how you get along on your own for a few days," Don called as we three climbed into the plane.

He got along. In fact, in his effort to please, Ramdat even did some things we hadn't asked him to do. Like burning down our grove of papaya and avocado trees. On our return from town, we spotted the charred area between the house and the river as Don came in for our landing.

"It could be worse," Don said, taxiing back from the end

of the runway. "At least the house is still standing."

Ramdat was waiting to help us carry the children and bags to the house. "Well, Ma'm," he smiled sheepishly. "I just set fire to the parched grass all around to clear the ground and surprise you and the master. It was a windy day."

"Well, Ramdat, you did surprise me and the master," I frowned, surveying the few papaya trees left closest to the house. Those that were destroyed had been heavy with fruit and I almost cried when next day a huge papaya, black and charred, dropped to the ground to show us how ripe and edible it had been.

We were sick about the loss of the avocados. We had purchased the grafts from the Georgetown Botanical Gardens almost a year before and had nursed them with exceeding care until they fruited.

As we unpacked, Don made an observation that never left us. "It's almost as if Ramdat has a button on the back of his head that regulates his brain. Sometimes it's *on*, but lots of times it's *off*." Don gave Ramdat a lecture on "thinking" that evening. Ramdat listened intently and smiled. But therein lay a problem. If he understood, he smiled. If he didn't, he'd smile, too.

Three days after the Great Fire, Ramdat's button was off again. This time he forgot to close the chicken coop. He knew that was important and had been doing it every night for three weeks, dutifully. But there was that button.

Sometime after midnight, we were awakened by an awful ruckus outside.

"Foxes!" Don yelled as I grabbed the flashlight and held it for him as he leaped into his shoes and grabbed his pistol. He took the light and ran.

I sat on the bed in the dark shivering and listening to shots and the terrified cackling of hens. It was many minutes before I heard Don's quick, determined step at the front door.

"How bad was it? I asked, fearfully.

"They got three laying hens and five baby chicks," he answered, angrily. "Ramdat didn't even wake up."

But when he had his button turned on, Ramdat was quite helpful. It took him an hour-and-a-half to wash dishes, sweep the floor, or set the table, but at least those assignments were done. He had a passion for neatness, which was satisfying because I'd once had it too. The kitchen sparkled, the pot and pans shone. If our little family went away for a day, Ramdat would usually surprise me by polishing all the "wares"—knives, forks and spoons— or cleaning the oven. Deductive reasoning was another matter.

"Ramdat, put some gas in the plane this morning, please," Don asked, as Ramdat cleared the breakfast dishes.

"Yessir!" he replied, with his usual grin.

"How much gas is left in the barrels?"

"None, Sir."

"None? Absolutely none?"

"That's right, Sir." A grin.

"Then Ramdat, how are you going to put gas in the plane this morning?"

Another grin.

It was Ramdat's job to start the water pumps once each day to fill our two drums that served as storage tanks for wash water. It got so he'd be gone thirty or forty minutes before we'd hear the distant buzzing of the pump down at the river.

"What in the world takes you so long, Ramdat?" I asked one day.

"Well, Ma'am, this morning it took me seventy-three

pulls before the motor would start," he replied, showing his pearly teeth.

"Don't you think there's something wrong with it then? I queried.

"Yes, Ma'am. *Long pause*. Should I tell the master?"

It was like that. If asked, he'd answer. But Ramdat was reluctant to offer any information. As we suffered in silence, we had to come up with the right questions.

We had trouble with our saltshaker after Ramdat came to Marquis. I'd take the dessicant out of the top, dry it in a warm oven, and then set in on the kitchen windowsill to stay dry until the next meal. It wasn't until I saw Ramdat taking it from there to soak in the sink that I understood the solid lump in the shaker at mealtime. *Today's lesson will be on the purpose of dessicants.*

Living so far away from civilization, Don and I were always conscientious about saving and conserving. But still there were things to be thrown away in pits dug away from the house. We burned what we could, but the pits filled up rapidly with both household refuse and the crew's trash. One day, a change in the direction of the wind told us our current pit was too full.

"When you're finished in the house today, Ramdat, would you start digging a new pit for the garbage? The other one is too full. You know where the shovels are," Don directed as he left for the barge. Ramdat replied with his inevitable grin and nod, finished the dishes, and went about his new assignment. He was nothing if not eager to please.

It took a few days, but Ramdat announced the new pit was finished. I ceased watching his labor from afar, congratulated him on a job well done, and promptly forgot about the new pit. A week or so later, another breeze brought unpleasant odors into the house.

"Maybe there's a dead capybara down by the river,"

Don surmised when I mentioned this at dinner. "I'll check in the morning." He did.

"Ramdat!" I heard Don's loud call next day. It sounded urgent so I went running, too.

"Are you trying to build a mountain of garbage to rival those?" Don was gesturing at the nearby hills. Ramdat thought this was funny and giggled. "Why in heaven's name aren't you using the new pit you finished last week?" The reply was Ramdatypical.

"Because you didn't tell me to, Sir." *Our mistake.*

We had given Ramdat permission to borrow any of our books and his choice of reading material astonished me. In fact, I suspected we had a budding genius as a house-boy, button or no.

"Last Sunday it was our *History of the Church* he went off with," I was telling Don as we both settled down to read on a Sunday afternoon. "And today it's *Merck's Medical Manual.*"

"Maybe there's hope after all," Don sighed, turning back to his 'Sunday paper," — *Air Facts* magazine.

The following Sunday, Ramdat went off with a book entitled *Childbirth. Could he be a budding OB/GYN?* But his favorite became the *Rubaiyat of Omar Khayyam.* Weeks went by, but Ramdat didn't trade the *Rubaiyat* for anything else. One morning I found both him and the broom leaning against the kitchen counter. Ramdat was studying the small leather-bound volume in front of him.

"But what does this really mean, Ma'am," he asked me.

I glanced down at the page and slowly began a simple discussion of the Persian poet's verses, philosophy, and allegory. It's always harder to explain something to someone else than to understand, so I'm sure I stumbled over my own thoughts as I talked. But I was impressed that he was interested and wondered aloud to Don that night that our house-boy might become a great East Indian philosopher. I could sense Don's smile in the darkness.

Don wandered into the kitchen next day as Ramdat sat reading the *Rubaiyat*, while waiting for the tea water to boil. I overheard part of a discussion on the distinction between lying, that is, the telling of untruths, and lying as one does on a bed.

"But which one does he mean when he writes 'under the dust he lies?" asked Ramdat.

With the addition of Ramdat to our household, life was not only easier for us but also more amusing during those dry months of "winter." Inevitably the rains would come. Just as inevitable was Ramdat's departure.

As we approached summer, he got chicken pox, we think. He also got the flu, we think. It was the first time he'd been sick since joining us, but he made up for lost time. Ramdat was *really* sick. His face radiated gloom, and we felt sick just to look at him. Doctor Don tried to diagnose his ailment, but that was difficult since, as Don poked and prodded, Ramdat responded 'yes' to every "does it hurt here?" and when asked to tell us how he felt, he described most of the symptoms in *Merck's Medical Manual.*

"That's going to be tough to diagnose, Dr. Don," I remarked. "His chills and fever indicate malaria. Maybe we should give him a full course of Aralen," I suggested, knowing we had this in our medicine chest.

"Unless it's typhoid fever, or appendicitis, or small pox," Don countered. I trembled, knowing baby Tom had not had his smallpox vaccination yet. From that moment on I diagnosed every cabourri bite on either Diney or Tom as the beginning of some pox.

We finally both agreed it was chicken pox. And flu. Ramdat was, of course, quarantined from everyone else. Confined to his hammock, he felt so miserable he shunned even the *Rubaiyat*. But when the pox stopped forming, we decided to fly him in to Georgetown to see a doctor.

"Take a week off with pay to recover," Don offered an almost recovered and much happier Ramdat. Instead of a thank you, Ramdat declared he wanted two weeks with pay and for us to come back to Georgetown and fetch him at the end of that time. We decided he wasn't all *that* indispensable and the last we saw of Ramdat was when we dropped him in Georgetown and headed for the Woodbine Hotel.

From there I phoned my friend Marie to see if she was still in B.G. She and her husband and children were scheduled to take "long leave" in the UK soon. They would be gone almost a year.

"No, Ma'am," answered Noreen, their African maid, in reply to my query. "Miz Lyder and the children left yesterday. The doctor he say he's gonna let me go tomorrow 'cuz he's leaving soon. You don't need anyone to work for you, do you Miz Haack?"

I could scarcely believe what I'd heard. "Need anyone!" I exclaimed. "Stay right where you are, Noreen. I'll be right over to talk to you. I'll bring the children—do you think you could watch them this afternoon while I do some shopping?"

This was too perfect! Noreen was out of a job for at least many months. If she wanted to leave Georgetown for the interior, we'd take her! I'd known Noreen as long as I had my friend, Marie. In the few times I'd left Diney with her while Marie and I did errands together in Georgetown, I'd seen a real love between them.

A few days later, Noreen in her ever-present wide brimmed black hat, climbed into the back seat of our plane. Baby Tom was on her lap. Diney snuggled against her side. Though she had never flown in a small plane before nor seen any of her country beyond Georgetown, fiftyish Noreen never batted an eye when she told us of her decision. She had no family to leave behind so she was free to begin her love affair with the interior and to dote on her two little charges who grew to adore her. From her first day at Marquis, Noreen was happily at home in isolation.

I had a new life! The children were whisked from their cribs as soon as they opened their eyes in the morning. Diapers were silently changed and Noreen and our two babies were gone from the house for an early morning stroll while I turned over in bed for a few more winks.

Noreen was a good cook, too. It was a joy to come home at dusk on the evening of mail plane day and find a fish dinner, brown and crisp, waiting for us as we walked in the house. Now I could join Don *every* Friday, at Good Hope or Lethem, to socialize and have a day out.

As November approached, Noreen asked for enough rum to soak her dried fruits in preparation for Christmas fruitcakes. This dark cake, heavy with raisins, citron, pineapple bits, and cherries was a "given" in Marie and Derek Lyder's home. Noreen implied it wouldn't be Christmas in our home without it.

"And just think," Don grinned as I raved to him about Noreen once again, "all this for only thirty-dollars a month."

Noreen was sitting on the living room couch, a child on either side, reading Dr. Seuss for the hundredth time. She loved the rhymes, the illustrations, the silliness of the stories as much as Diney and Tom did.

I don't know who was happier then, Don, Noreen, Diana and Tom, or I. Could it last?

15

Menagerie

O ur family's definition of domestic animals differed from the norm. Beginning with Chibi, we came to love a number of four-legged creatures, some more than others. Don and I regretted having to leave Chibi behind in the 'States at the beginning of our adventure. So, we looked forward to having other pets just as soon as we were in our own home. Of course once there, we found some creatures would slither or creep into the house uninvited. These were shown little hospitality. We both loved animals, but I had my limits.

I've described how I acquired "Tigger" at a plane stop at Karanambo and how while we tried to love him, he definitely held no affection for us. It was only our first encounter with a wild cat which wanted to stay wild.

Don's brother, Bob, visited the Rupununi during our house building and decided he, too, should have an ocelot to take back to the 'States with him. Don and I did not encourage him, but he passed the word around the savannah and it wasn't long before an Indian presented him with a "baby" ocelot.

"A leetle bebe. She very quiet," Pedro announced.

Bob and Don promptly flew the crate and its occupant

from Good Hope to our partially constructed house at Marquis where they could let it loose since, at that stage, the doors were on and the windows screened. Carefully, they pried off one side of the crate and stood back. Fortunately.

"Jesus!" Bob exclaimed as a snarling, spitting adolescent ocelot sprang from the crate and headed for the nearest corner. It was a replay of my adventure in the Woodbine Hotel. Bob advanced, the ocelot snarled and spat. Don reached out with soothing words and was met with hostility. Both brothers hung their hammocks in the barracoun that night.

The next morning, their entrance through the front door startled the ocelot. In a flash it gave a mighty leap and landed on top of the eight-foot high living room wall. Bob began to have second and third thoughts about taking this particular "pet" back to Milwaukee and called to our crew for help. A grand effort on the part of all comers who poked, prodded, and lured with raw meat finally got the ocelot down from the wall—and out the open front door. The collective sigh of relief was lead by Bob and not a tear was shed at the loss.

After we moved into our house, we felt it wouldn't be complete without a dog. Thus, when a visitor offered us a mongrel pup, we took it gladly. These "gifts" of animals usually entailed an exchange of goods from our shop down by the barracoun. The Indians obviously "knew our number."

But "Mike" was cuter as a puppy than as a grown dog, having the decided disadvantage of getting dumber as he grew up. It was as if, in the growing process, his brain went in reverse. He was a car-chaser type dog. But at Marquis, we didn't have any cars. So Mike took to chasing Don's plane, not on take-off, when the engine noise frightened him away. But as the plane returned and drifted silently toward the airstrip, it would catch Mike's eye and he would be off for the chase. Several of us would run from the house or the barracoun to yell and warn him away, but Mike was courting disaster and refused to give up his bad habit. Biting tires on a car is dangerous, biting a feathering propeller is suicide and of course the day came when he lost the game.

Our chickens didn't fall into the pet category, but we loved them nonetheless for what they produced, *when* they produced. *Only* for what they produced. Which was never enough. With fresh meat and milk nearly non-existent, we relied on eggs for many of our meals. I used them as fast as they were laid, my biggest dilemma being whether to use the three available for a cake or for breakfast.

When they weren't laying, wise old Dutch said the 'schickens' were just "wanting to set."

"They aren't getting enough to eat," offered Nellie.

"It's too wet for them to lay," said Caesar after a couple of heavy rains.

Or it was too dry in the dry season. Or they just finished hatching a brood and wouldn't lay for another month. A dropped egg in our house was a large-scale tragedy.

Dutch was very fond of chicken, fried, stewed, or in a casserole. He kept urging us to eat some of the cocks so that the hens could have a rest and a chance to lay some eggs. That was another reason.

"That's why they don't lay, ya know," he offered.

So we ate chicken and we ate chicken until one day we discovered there wasn't a single cock left in the chicken yard. *Now I suppose the chickens won't lay because their lives are so uninteresting.*

"Bambi" was our dearest pet. We traded with a Brazilian for this tiny fawn which had no trouble finding its way into our hearts. Diney could feed Bambi with formula from a baby bottle and Tommy, who was just learning to stand

Diney feeding Bambi

up, could "crawl up" Bambi until he stood on his own two feet.

At first Bambi preferred sleeping on the cool floor of our dark bedroom closet. Don and I cautioned the children not to startle him so that he could become accustomed to being around people. He took his milk greedily but still seemed to be frightened all the time.

"Bambi just doesn't seem very happy, Don," I said after a week. Both of us knew wild animals should stay in the wild, but in Bambi's case, that was dangerous. The Brazilian who'd brought him to us had shot the mother for camp meat. We were Bambi's only "family."

"Let's let him go free then," Don said sadly. "Maybe he'll stay around the compound where we can all protect him."

A few disappointing days passed without our spotting our dear Bambi. The children were tearful. Don and I were sad. We were sure we'd lost our little friend and tried to console ourselves that Bambi was making his own way in his natural world. Then one afternoon I was at the counter in the kitchen when I spotted something moving among the papaya trees. Quickly I turned to warm some milk on the stove and fill the baby bottle.

Both children were napping so I slipped quietly out the kitchen door. Moving slowly toward the papaya grove, I called Bambi's name, softly. He stood tensed, ready to bolt at the slightest provocation. I held my breath and slowly held out his bottle. The smell of warm milk overcame his timidity, and he walked haltingly toward me to take the bottle in his mouth and suck. I was ecstatic!

Bambi came every day thereafter until we left Marquis for good. Each afternoon he'd whimper outside the front door until someone let him in. His tiny hooves clicked gaily on the smooth cement floor as he headed for surer footing on the fiber rug. Diana and Tommy were full of joy each time Bambi showed up and amazingly, as we all got used to each other, Bambi never minded having his ears pulled or the hugs each of us gave him. He didn't scratch, bite, bark, or sting and never left a mess in the house. How perfect a pet could you have? And he loved watermelon, as much as Diney loved feeding it to him.

Don put out the word in our territory that no one was to harm Bambi. We put a red collar on him so that he'd be recognizable and watched as his spots disappeared over time. He grew strong on his daily pint of milk and watermelon and Diney soon discovered he loved both apple pie and papaya. Not a diet a vet would recommend, but Bambi was one happy and healthy deer. Even after we felt on his head— the hard little knobs that would become antlers— Bambi stayed with us in Marquis valley.

Someone brought us an accouri, and we took it in, too. This hairy little creature, the size of a full-grown squirrel or rat actually made a noise like a Great Dane growling. But it seemed harmless, and after we determined that it didn't bite, the children were intrigued. What the accouri *did* fancy was a diet of wood.

We'd had him only a few days when I found him gnawing away on our beautiful redwood windowsill.

"This creature has got to go!" I told Don vehemently. Don agreed, all too easily.

"Ramdat!" he called. Take this animal and give him to the Indian children down at the barracoun." We didn't care where he went, just so long as it was somewhere else.

This was on a morning when we were all to fly out to Karanambo for a short visit with the McTurks. But weather closed in and we were forced to stay the night with Connie and Tiny. When we got home next day, the house was a minor wreck.

"I just thought I'd leave him in the house for a while, Ma'am," Ramdat explained. "I guess I forgot about him."

So we were minus two deerskin rugs in the children's room, the wooden mallet for their hammer toy, the handle for my meat grinder, nine-tenths of a one pound tin of butter which had been left open in the pantry, and the rest of the dining room windowsill. Wanting to wring Ramdat's neck, I would have settled for the accouri's. . . if I'd have caught him.

"Ramdat," I growled through my teeth.

"I'm going Ma'am," he said, catching the accouri as it eyed a tasty morsel of another windowsill. He made haste with the wretched little beast, out the kitchen door.

Amongst the ones we wanted there were plenty of creatures we didn't. No matter how Don tried to persuade me that all snakes were not *bad*, as far as I was concerned they were. They silently went about their mission to kill me with fright, beginning with the one that dropped down from under the windowsill onto my dinner plate the first night in our new house.

Dutch, Harry, Don, and I were sitting on stools eating at the kitchen counter side by side, so our unexpected visitor had a choice of whose plate he would decorate.

"Agh! I choked, knocking over my stool as I jumped back from the counter. Without a word, the three men dispatched the snake and resumed eating.

"Yup," Dutch muttered. "Dat's a bad vun." Which, the others explained as I reluctantly walked back into the kitchen, was a 'Labaria," the local name for our Fer-de-Lance.

Shortly after the dinner plate episode, I was cleaning the shower in our bathroom. This room wasn't quite finished, so until the men sloped the floor *toward* the outside wall drain and put a screen on it to keep out critters, we discouraged them with a square oil can in front of the hole.

Mop in hand, I reached down, pulled the can away and out rolled three huge coils of snake. All powers of speech left me. I jumped back and stood transfixed. Diney was asleep in our bedroom. Should I run for help? Should I stay there and...do what?

I decided on action—run for help.

"Harry! Don! Come fast! Help!" I shouted, retrieving my voice as I ran towards the barracoun and its nearby machine shop.

Both Harry and Don came running. My wide-eyed white face told them this was serious. The three of us passed our still-sleeping baby and descended on the snake. That is, Harry and Don descended on it, as I watched from a safe distance.

"Oh, it's only a baby anaconda," observed Harry, as he tried shoving the loathsome creature back through the drain hole. " It's a constrictor type snake, Jan, it wouldn't have hurt you. They can get up to twenty-five feet when they're grown."

"Baby! Three feet long?" I retorted, near tears. "I want that drain screened *now!*" I demanded. "That 'baby' *could* have killed me! I nearly had a heart attack!" Now I was mad at the lack of sympathy I was getting. They recognized anger when they saw it and promptly set to work screening the drain hole.

It took some time to "snake-proof" the house, and I was never convinced that it was totally secure from reptiles. I wished I were as blasé about snakes as Don was. But even that was about to change.

One evening after dinner and putting Diney to bed, Don worked by the light of a Tilley lamp at the desk in the room that served as our "office", one step down from our bedroom. I sat on the step keeping him company, my bare feet on the floor, my skirt draped over the step.

Don turned his head toward me and said in a serious tone,

"Jan. Don't move."

Without hesitation, I jumped back and landed halfway into the bedroom behind me. The snake that had been crossing my skirt flew off onto the office floor. Where, with surprising haste and vigor, Don smashed the loathsome intruder to a pulp with the wooden bench. When he looked back up at me, his face was pale.

"Now who's afraid of snakes," I chided. "Compared to 'Jumbo' in the shower this one was tiny. It couldn't have been more than a foot long!"

Don had trouble controlling the tremor in his voice.

"Jan, that small snake was a coral snake. Its venom is a nerve poison. It's one of the most dangerous snakes we have around here."

Fortunately the pulpy mess on the floor *was* the only coral snake we ever saw at our house or anywhere else in the Rupununi.

Don taught the children not to be afraid of snakes. I taught them to keep a sharp eye out for them and never, never to go near one. If they saw a snake, they were not to move and to call someone for help.

In our years at Marquis Don had a close call with a rattler, both of us—on separate occasions—with bushmasters. Luckily we never had occasion to open our snake bite kit, though it was always at the ready.

The uninvited local talent included scorpions, iguanas, and frogs. The ugly iguanas took up residence near the chicken coop, but scorpions found their way into the house and could be found in piles of linens, underwear, and shoes.

"These frogs will drive me nuts!" I remarked to Don, as I finished my daily shower.

"I know; no privacy at all," he sympathized.

It wasn't privacy I was seeking. It was the intermittent "whack" and feel of little frog suction feet on my backside that I loathed. No amount of frantic gyrations dislodged them. My showers were always punctuated with small screams and disgusted *yucks*.

Dutch traded some dry goods at our store for a small monkey we named "Jocko." Diana and Tommy loved stuffing him full of soda crackers, and of course Jocko provided us with no end of entertainment. Don constructed a home for him under the water tank platform outside. It was, at least in one respect, an improvement on our own house. Jocko's home had a drop-down shower curtain which kept the blowing rains from his dinners. The soda crackers stayed dry in the fiercest weather.

We also shared our valley with an extended family of Capybaras, the largest of the rodent family, sometimes weighing as much as three hundred pounds. Looking like a cross between a pig and a rat, they devastated our corn crop each year and were the bane of Dutch's existence. He was determined to save at least some of the corn for his 'schickens.' The Brazilians and Indians ate Capybara and Nellie told us it tasted much like pork.

The summer we traveled to the 'States for Tommy's birth, we left Dutch in charge of the house and compound. The corn was high and the capybaras eagerly awaited each midnight when they could run rampant through the cornfield, helping themselves to tender cobs and trampling all else. We'd left Dutch with a shotgun to scare them away, but since it was dark as pitch outside and Dutch was deaf as a post, this was only a hopeful plan. Besides, Dutch usually retired immediately after sundown. In the three months we were gone, Dutch used six boxes of shotgun shells. But we four came back to a demolished cornfield and, somewhere out there, an entire herd of fat, happy capybara.

It was Dutch and his 'schickens' that were unhappy. So we added 'feed corn' to our list of provisions to be shipped from Georgetown. The price of eggs had just gone up at Marquis. .

16

On Her Majesty's Post

In those days before e-mail and satellite phones, our solitude was joyously punctuated by "mail plane day," Fridays, when the DC-3 arrived at Good Hope or, on alternate Fridays, at Lethem. On almost every Friday from 1955 to the end of 1958 ten or twelve letters left Marquis, assuring families that we were still alive, stockholders that we were still laboring, and friends that we had just survived another hair-raising adventure.

My mother and father wanted no part of my glorious descriptions of our home and life in the jungle. They required information on what little Diana had added to her vocabulary that week, whether Tommy was crawling as yet and, incidentally, why didn't we come "home."

"The Michigan U tee shirt fits Tommy perfectly," I'd write, ignoring both the questions and omitting our latest adventure, sane and mild as it had been. Mother and Dad had already decided that our lives were all in peril so my letters to them were of the mundane to convince them we were a "normal" family, however displaced.

Their arguments were unceasing and, sometimes, outlandish. When America's tiff with Great Britain over the Suez Canal was in the news, Dad predicted that it wouldn't be long before we were at war with that country.

"Even if you don't care," he wrote sarcastically, "I'd just as soon my grandchildren don't grow up in an orphanage while you and Don waste away in a British internment camp." I wrote back, explaining we were within swimming distance from Brazil across the river, even if authorities *could* get through to seize us without hiring our plane to accomplish this. "Our friends in Brazil will see that we're safe from British enemies, should it come to that." Of course, it didn't.

My letters to Don's family took a different tone. While I regaled them with tales of their brilliant grandchildren, I also included colorful descriptions of encounters with snakes and scorpions, the latest episodes involving our crew, and visitors to our compound, and a few—sadly only a few—tales of diamond strikes in the Ireng River. These were the tasty bits they loved passing on to their friends and other relatives to reinforce how brave and venturesome we were.

Letters to friends depended on which friends they were. With Marilyn and Ray we'd stress the dryness of the season and the martinis. To Don's old college roommates, John and Doug, Don would go into minute detail of each snake, each pocket of diamonds in the river, and every near catastrophe with our small plane.

To my friends Judy and Linda, I'd complain about having to bake bread, haul water, count rough diamonds, learn how to speak Brazilian in order to deal with our numerous servants, and occasionally fight off anacondas in the shower.

During the year between my graduation, our wedding, and our departure for South America, I'd done some radio interviews with Esther Hotton on WTMJ in Milwaukee. This was in connection with my job as a marketing specialist for the county extension agency. Esther and I liked each other, and she eagerly followed our experiences from the beginning. She felt her radio audience would be interested in my new life and asked that I write her about it. Many were the nights I spent perched on a trusty packing box in front of my typewriter composing the latest installment of "Jungle Mother" for Esther.

Our agent in town, Alan DeSouza, collected our incoming mail to forward to Good Hope or Lethem. From the start, it contained numerous packages from my parents, designed mostly to keep their grandchildren from being underprivileged. If the goodies tempted me to return to civilization, leaving behind the barbarian who forced me to live in the jungle with him, so much the better. Mother was spending a small fortune on ruffled sun suits, size 2, but I admit, her packages helped enormously to make life more fun, even if I did have to pay 33% duty on everything cleared through Her Majesty's Customs.

When I was in Georgetown and received a pink slip in our mailbox indicating a package awaited, I looked forward to a full morning to clear it and the loss of several fingernails since Mother was the world's best package-wrapper. The customs clerk, with infuriating calm, would watch me struggle with the package while a long queue of hot impatient people waited behind me. Eventually I'd succeed with the opening for inspection and, with sparks shooting from my eyes, would shove it across the counter at the clerk. Almost motionless, he would glance down at the contents (which had been neatly noted on the *outside* of the package), raise an eyebrow and say "Now package it back, if you please, Mistress, and step to the next window." Where I forked over the 33% duty.

Time was always of the essence on our trips to Georgetown. Either we'd left the children with Nellie at Good Hope or had Marie or Pam's maid baby- sitting for an afternoon as we rushed to do our errands. Once in a while I lost my 25% Irish temper with a particularly supercilious customs clerk. This happened when I was clearing a package for Don that was clearly marked "Spare Motor Parts" on the outside.

"What kind of motor parts are these, Mistress," the clerk asked.

"They're for my husband's plane," I offered, guessing.

"Please open it and we'll see."

I looked at the little box. No string. No tape. Just quarter inch cardboard, glued fast, then stapled. Impenetrable. I was hot and short on time. I thought of my fingernails and decided I wasn't going down without a fight.

"When I *do* get it open," I began sweetly, "do you think you will be able to tell if they are spare parts for a plane, a boat, or a suction dredge?"

"The package *please*, Mistress."

I had, at least, ruffled the sphinx.

"I know how they get to be customs clerks," I complained to Don later that day. "They major in How to Enjoy Human Suffering and minor in Spoiling Surprises at Christmas."

Don smiled. It didn't bother *him* that we not only had to describe in detail on the outside of each Christmas package we sent but also wrote for all to see the exact worth of the item.

I had but one triumph, the memory of which I thrived on for many months. On Diana's birthday my parents sent three huge packages filled to bursting with all sorts of lovely things to wear or play with. These and a fourth from one of my friends were listed, curiously, on one pink slip. Normally there would be a pink slip for each. It was almost teatime when I got to the customs desk, which was even more swamped than usual. Mass frustration gripped clerks and customers alike, and in the midst of it, I managed to get out all four packages for the small duty on one. It was, indeed, a triumphant day.

The Christmas presents we asked for were more practical than costly: Toll House Cookie Mix, popping corn, and Graham Cracker crumbs among them. Somewhere I had read that one could make "snow" from Tide, so I asked for that, too, hoping it wouldn't be crushed and distributed throughout the rest of the package contents. That had happened once with Comet cleanser, so that our cakes made from mixes tasted faintly of chlorine for months following.

Diney and I made our own "snow" that Christmas from boxes of Tide and two drops of water so a snowman and snow lady graced center of the dining room table at Marquis. Since the children had never seen snow, the whole concept was probably lost on them, but it satisfied me. We sent Don in search of a Christmas tree while we made paper chains and aluminum foil stars. He returned with a good, full tree, which was about as far removed from the spruce and pine families as botany permits.

"But it has its own red berries," he said proudly. "So my decorating is done."

My dad must have given Mother free rein that Christmas. We received our "practical presents," plus gifts designed to keep us from going completely native. One box contained three lacy slips, three pair of nylons, a bottle of Tabou perfume, a Georges Briard cooking utensil –which never came within ten feet of The Stove—a pair of black lace panties (from my mother?), a yellow silk nightgown, a compact, and lipstick. Don's box held bourbon and books.

The "care packages" kept us happy, but it was my invasion of the all-male bastion of Her Majesty's Customs warehouse that provided a soul-satisfying benchmark in our life in British Guiana. Whether or not I was the first female to invade this territory, I don't know. But I did discover the mere presence of a female in this locale was like unto the wave of a magic wand, subduing the confusion and noise of ill-mannered male against angry ill-mannered male.

I didn't go Her Majesty's Customs warehouse often, but when I did, from the moment I stepped over the threshold of that cavernous building the scramble was on to save me from being trampled in the chaos. The man who had been at the head of the line dropped back to give me his place at the window.

"Eh, eh Mon. Don't you see dere's a laydee here? You all go back deh wheh you belongs."

"Eh, dere. Who you shovin'? Give de laydee room, nah?"

I greased no palms. I smiled and said thank you to each gentleman in turn. It was amazing. Even the customs clerk was flustered enough to join the others' chivalry. I like to think that, at least in this respect, Guyana is different from the British Guiana we knew. It makes me smile to think there are several women entering Her Majesty's Customs on a daily basis. Perhaps the chivalry is still there.

17

Side Trips

O ur most immediate neighbors—the ones only ten miles away—were Macusi Indians and they didn't speak English. Don and I learned enough of the Macusi tongue for basic communication, but friendly conversation was out of reach.

Nellie and Caesar Gorinsky, fifteen flying minutes away, were our closest friends and most of our trips away from home were to Good Hope. Diney and their five-year-old Christopher were playmates, so we tried to get them together at least once a week. The mail plane landed at Good Hope every other Friday and very few things could prevent me from going with Don to meet it. On "Lethem Fridays" Don would drop me and the children at Good Hope and go on alone or with Caesar, to Lethem where they'd collect mail, cargo, and gossip.

Nellie and I began our visit with a cup of tea, chattering like magpies for half an hour. Since the previous Friday neither of us had had access to a receptive ear for the telling of things that interested *us*. After clearing the list of the children's bumps, scrapes and accomplishments, the happenings with the diamond dredge, we'd slow down to discuss the various scandals occurring in the savannahs or the ones that showed potential. Nellie was a dear, dear friend, combination of mother, sister, confidant. She was, in both my and Don's opinion, the very best mentor-to-get-stuck-with-for-three-years-in-the-jungle. I was lucky to have her closest to me and wondered if Don would have dared take me to British Guiana had he not met, admired and loved Nellie.

On one of his many flights downriver to Good Hope and Lethem, Don discovered a pristine little lake in Brazil, across the Ireng River. Once discovered, it became "our lake" though it already had the name "Cara Cara Na" and belonged to an old Brazilian everyone called "Tenient Cicero." He had been a lieutenant in some army during some war and the title stuck. "Tenient" loved company, especially when it produced a bottle of rum. In our case, it always did.

Cara Cara Na was Tenient's "out station" where his vaqueros stayed. There was an old cabin there for them but it took years before old Tenient realized that this area was so beautiful that he should make his own home there. Certainly the scenery with its perfectly round little lake rimmed with white sand and surrounded by huge cashew trees was wasted on the cattle. Tenient built his house in the midst of a nearby citrus grove, constructed an airstrip for small aircraft and added a tiny blue and white chapel and house for the visiting Padre.

With such a spot within eight minutes' flight from Good Hope, the Gorinskys and Haacks had a great day trip destination. Don and I would pack Diana and Tommy into the plane, fly to Good Hope, wedge Caesar, Nellie and little Chris amongst the fried chicken, lemonade jugs, flippers, masks, inner tubes and a lattice-work of fishing rods and be off for a day in Paradise. With all that stuff, surely we were " happy crampers."

The lake itself was about a mile across, almost perfectly round. Its white sandy beach was shaded by lovely old cashew trees, perfectly spaced for hanging hammocks. After a day of feasting and swimming, Don and I would lie in our big Brazilian double hammock and plan a small resort alongside the lake. But then, one day we discovered a small drawback to this plan: the lake was filled with piranhas.

Caesar and Don discovered them on one trip—I think our last—when they took an old leaky dugout across to the side opposite to where Nellie and I and the children were splashing about just off the beach. The two of them hoped to find lukanani—a wonderful tasty fish that we all loved.

Time after time Don or Caesar would cast while the other steadied the tippy dugout with a paddle. They got strikes, short stuggles, but then lost the fish.

Don's last cast hooked a fat lukanani, which gave him a good fight for half a minute. Then his line suddenly whipped in with only a fish head attached to it. Don and Caesar looked long and hard at the head, then at each other and slowly, carefully picked up their paddles and headed the leaky craft slowly back toward our shore.

"Get the children out," Caesar shouted, as they got near. "Get out!"

Safe on the beach, they told us what had happened. We could scarcely believe our perfect spot actually had a fault. A serious fault. *Well, there goes our idea for a resort.*

It was a bad scare, which served to dampen, if not kill, our enthusiasm for Cara Cara Na.

Nellie and I dragged the waterlogged, water-wrinkled, sunburnt and exhausted children from the shallow water where they'd been playing and gathered up the remnants of our picnic. It was always a trick to time our return flight to manage "dumping" the Gorinsky family on Good Hope airstrip and still get home to Marquis before darkness fell, which it does quickly that near the Equator.

Our other favorite "neighbors" were Connie and Tiny McTurk, both British subjects but Rupununi-ites for a lifetime. Their ranch, Karanambo, was as far away from Marquis as Nellie and Caesar's "Good Hope"—in a different direction. On a Sunday we'd often fly over to visit them, strategically arriving at teatime. *Oh, is it teatime? Please don't bother with anything special for us.*

Connie, a spare little woman whose khaki shirts and trousers always seemed a few sizes too large, would smile warmly, step out to the kitchen to have a word with her cook, Antone, and then join Tiny, Don and me for conversation. Her grandchildren were miles away so she took delight in watching Diana and Tommy and their antics. Don and Tiny were cut from the same cloth: rugged individualists who enjoyed life's challenges and stood ready to shape their world to their order.

Soon a lovely "tea" would be spread on the long plank, which served as a dining room table in the half-walled room at the front of the house. The "dining room," like the other rooms in the house, didn't have a proper floor. But the hard packed soil under our feet was kept tidy with a broom of rushes and the plank table was set with England's finest bone china. We all sat on the packing crates which served as chairs and thoroughly enjoyed hot rolls spread with homemade jam, delicious custard (for which Antone was renowned), guava jelly, hot, strong English tea and a light-as-a-feather jellyroll. Connie and Tiny's "schickens" obviously did a better job of producing eggs than ours did.

Diana and Tommy loved playing with the pigs and chickens running in and out of the house and would laugh with delight when two or three of the McTurk's tame birds would land on their shoulders. Diney and her little pail of corn would soon have a flock of chickens surrounding her.

An impressive array of fishing poles, Indian handicrafts, king-sized beetles mounted on soft boards, bows and arrows and hooks for hammocks covered what small portions of walls there were. The main bedroom had five beds in it and often they were all spoken for, either by Connie and Tiny's elder daughter and her children visiting from Georgetown, guests like us, or paying guests from town who'd come for peace and quiet and the best fishing in the country.

Two kitchens and a large garage completed the compound. In the smaller of the two kitchens Connie created her masterpieces while Antone ruled the outdoor kitchen preparing feasts of roast duck or baked chicken, each with a gravy made from pounds of butter. Still Connie and Tiny were as thin as rails, browned by the sun and healthy as Rupununi horses.

Over New Year's of 1957-58, Dutch, the children, Don and I flew over to Karanambo, at Tiny and Connie's invitation, for a fishing trip. We packed our small plane with a playpen mat, diapers, "Infanseat", and a few gifts from our shop, arriving, of course, just about tea time. Connie and I swung in hammocks watching the children play after tea while Don, Tiny and Dutch went duck hunting.

"We didn't get any," reported Tiny on their return. " But we had a lot of fun anyway." Tall and thin, tanned and dressed in the requisite, rumpled khaki pants and shirt, Tiny would not be described as handsome. But the merry twinkle in his eyes endeared him to everyone. The slouch felt hat, much like Dutch's, completed his persona.

Early the next morning Don, Dutch, Tiny and I drove off for the Simuni River, leaving Diana and Tommy with Connie. At the river's edge the four of us clambered into a large, wooden, flat bottomed boat, which in its other life was used to gather balata (raw rubber) -producing trees. A small engine on the back ran at low speed as we traveled up the river trolling for lukanani as we went. Before five minutes passed Don caught a big lukanani and then another and another.

"I don't seem to have any luck," I pouted, just as a fish took my line and began to struggle. "Help, oh help!" I gasped, trying to remember what I'd learned about reeling in a catch. "Look at him!" He's huge!" I yelled, reeling in the first fish I'd ever caught. I was so excited I nearly hugged the four-and-a-half-pound lukanani dangling at the end of my line. All of a sudden my luck changed and I began reeling in one lukanani after another. When we got to the widest part of the river, Don tried the casting rod and reeled in the biggest catch of the day, a six-and-a -half pounder, winning the prize.

My own pride wasn't dampened. When we got back to Karanambo I was fairly bursting with the excitement of catching *seven* fish. Antone, too, was overjoyed at the prospect of preparing a magnificent feast for all of us. While he disappeared to start melting the butter and the Indians expertly cleaned our catch, Tiny and Connie easily talked the rest of us into staying another night.

"We'll try our duck hunting again early tomorrow," directed Tiny. Now *that* pronouncement put a smile on all the men's faces. Even bigger smiles following the hunt the next morning when they returned with several ducks as their prize.

"It's been a *wonderful* stay!" I said happily to Connie and Tiny as we packed the plane with baskets of oranges and limes, some cold chicken, the remaining fish we'd caught, properly iced down, and two little children who were as loathe to leave as we were.

We were back at Karanambo some months later and found a film crew just ready to leave after taking footage for "Green Mansions." They had hoped to get film of bloodthirsty piranha devouring a live animal, but the little fish had not obliged. Of course we *could* have told them about Cara Cara Na, but that was still considered "our lake" so we stayed silent.

The month before we left Marquis for good, Don's mother and Dad visited us and, among other activities, we planned a fishing trip to the Simuni River with Tiny McTurk. The Arapaima, we were told, was the largest freshwater scale fish in the world. The fishing would take the entire day and the children were included. So we rigged a small hammock for them in the large "balata boat" carrying Don's mom, Connie McTurk, Don and his dad and me. Tiny led the way in a small boat powered by an outboard and we trailed two dugouts carrying Indians who would help with "the heavy work"—whatever that was to be. We made a colorful procession working our way upriver under the overhanging trees and vines.

Along the way we once again trolled for lukanani and between us managed to haul in fifteen, in assorted sizes. Don's mom squealed with delight each time fish was snagged. His dad, too, was having the time of his life and I could almost hear the tales he would tell when he got back to Milwaukee.

Once in the "Arapaima pool" the men divided themselves into the two dugouts, setting out six lines baited with Arawhana, the Arapaima's favorite food but which none of us humans liked. I readied the video camera –none too soon.

"We've hooked one!" shouted Don from the dugout he shared with Tiny. I focused on them just as the enormous fish tugged on the line, whipping their dugout around for a merry trip down river and then around in circle. I was so excited I didn't even notice the children idly plunking the lens caps into the water and watching them sink.

Eleanor, Erwin, Tiny with arapaima

"I'll get 'im now," called Tiny after several minutes of this merry-go-'round. The Arapaima had finally tired. Tiny raised his harpoon and drove it deep. The rest of us in our boat, though witnesses to the struggle, could scarcely believe our eyes as Don and Tiny paddled the dugout back to us. Later, when the Indians hoisted the fish up on the stout limb of a tree, it measured seven and a half feet long. Tiny, who was an expert at this, guessed his weight at about 175 pounds.

It was dark by now and the Indians let the Arapaima down to begin gutting and cleaning him.

"It's a harmless fish," Tiny explained, shining his flashlight on a row of tiny, soft teeth in the Arapaima's mouth. The Indians continued their cleaning and salting, completely in the dark, as the rest of us made our way back to Karanambo.

Now *that* was an adventure! Don's mother and dad were awed by it and could hardly wait to get home and spin the tale to their friends.

With the exception of Tiny and Connie McTurk, most of the Rupununi savannah was populated by Melville's— Nellie's brothers, sisters, and their families. Nellie and Caesar owned and operated Good Hope, Amy (Melville) and Ben Hart had Perara, Maggie (Melville) Orella ran Manari, Teddy Melville owned the hotel in Lethem, and so on and on. The story goes that the patriarch, Henry Percival Charles Melville ("HPC") ventured to British Guyana to find his fortune. There, in the South Savannah, he fell ill. Whether this was before or after the Wapishana Indians kidnapped him is not quite clear, but two of the Indian women nursed him back to health. Grateful for his recovered health, HPC married them both. These two women were Coco Mary and Coco Janet and between them they bore HPC twelve

children, Nellie, Amy, Maggie, Gina, John, Teddy, Lolly,
—the names go on. We never met them all.

Amy and Ben's ranch, Perara, was also on our visiting
list. An hour's jeep ride south of Good Hope, Perara was on
the way to Lethem. Ben Hart had been raised in Wisconsin
and like so many others we knew in British Guiana, left
home in search of his fortune. He and Amy were cattle
ranchers, raising also a few head of sheep and some pigs,
plus the requisite chickens. When Don and I tired of our
beef diet, we'd find an excuse to stop at Perara and buy
some pork or mutton from the Harts.

Situated on a lovely little creek, Perara had no cabourri
flies, so a swim there was a welcome treat for all of us. The
fishing was good too so it was to Perara that Nellie and
Caesar took us several times soon after our arrival in British
Guiana. An added bonus were the hours we spent listening
to the tales of settling the savannah.

Lethem, on the other hand, was a real "town." A
government "out station", Lethem had a population of
approximately 150 people. There was a hotel there, a store,
a bar, and the office of the District Commissioner, Eric
Cossou, a fine gentleman, a meticulous administrator. He
stood tall and ramrod straight, his formal bearing belying
a quiet sense of humor. He became a good and trusted
friend.

It was at Lethem that everyone congregated on alternate
Fridays to meet the mail plane and gossip about the latest
doings across the savannah. When Connie and Tiny's
daughter, Diane, was married in Lethem, the whole town,
plus surrounding ranchers and their families turned out
for the reception. Dutch was there, with his teeth *in* for
a change. Don and I and the children were invited to
overnight at "Government House," Eric Cossou's residence
where the reception was held. Brazilians, Indians, ranchers,

and the rest of us danced far into the night, after consuming cake and champagne. Diana and Tommy slept through it all in the room above the merriment.

Since we had the airplane, our visits to neighbors could not easily be returned. We did invite the McTurks to help us celebrate one of our anniversaries and Nellie and little Chris would fly in with Don for our children's birthday celebrations. Once in a while a small plane would land with an American or British stranger seeking company, a cool Scotch and soda and a clean comfortable hammock. Occasionally a young couple would appear in a small plane, eager to press us for advice on setting up a ranch, a dairy farm, a resort. We welcomed the company and the conversation and gave honest answers to all queries. Life would have been dull without these unexpected visits.

But no journey could ever surpass our flight to the southern-most tip of British Guiana for a stay with the Wai Wai tribe there. Don had twice previously flown down to this area bordering Brazil: to fly out a group of men whose plane had crashed near the village of this, the most primitive Indian tribe in B.G. and then again to take a woman missionary in for a stay of a few weeks with them. A missionary family had managed to live there in an attempt to bring Christianity into the lives of the Wai Wais who had previously been untouched by civilization. On the second visit, Don cleared it with the missionary family to bring me and one-year-old Diana with him on the trip to retrieve Mrs. Pryor.

"Of course we'll go with you!" I answered when Don posed the question of our visit. I'd listened with fascination to the tales of his previous trip. I knew any danger would not come from the Indians themselves, but from the flight's challenges. The Wai Wai's were two hundred and fifty miles away from Marquis. The range of our Tri-Pacer was more than that on full tanks of gas. But Don would want the gauges to read as close to "empty" as possible on landing at the short strip the Indians had carved out of the jungle next to their village. The plane would be at its lightest for landing and take-off with just enough gas left to reach Don's gasoline drums stored at Lumid Pau about ninety miles away on the trip back.

Sitting beside Don in the front seat, Diana on my lap, I searched the dark green of the jungle below for any sign of a clearing in the mass of trees. I held my breath as I finally sighted the airstrip, a narrow clearing near a group of thatched huts.

"Landing is going to be easier than taking off with one more person," Don said, checking his airspeed and pulling back on the joystick. "I think I'll ask the Indians to clear another ten feet of trees and underbrush before we have to leave."

The arrival of our plane was an event and the entire tribe, men, women with babies in slings and toddlers by their sides, and happy children scampering ahead of them all. The bare breasts I expected and was grateful for the strategically placed beaded square slung from a thong around the hips of both the men and the women. *A little modesty goes a long way.*

What stopped the surge of welcoming Indians was the sight of me carrying a blonde, blue-eyed baby. Diana took them all in with her wide China-blue eyes. Though Don remembers that I willingly allowed her to be passed from Indian woman to Indian woman, I remember some reluctance on my part, perhaps fearing the paint on their bodies might rub off on my precious child and I'd not be able to remove it.

We said grace before supper with the Hawkins family and Mrs. Pryor, the Wai Wai's staring in through the

Wai wai children

Wai wai elder

screens, listening with rapt attention as passages from the Bible were read. Then everyone joined in singing a hymn in Wai Wai language. After supper the men went to tie their hammocks under the house while Mrs. Hawkins, Mrs. Pryor and I sat on a big bed in the master bedroom and talked. Diana shared a crib that night with the Hawkins' twin daughters who were less than a year old. I watched as Mrs. Hawkins put her hair up in pincurls for the night while telling me a little about the Wai Wai's, their customs and beliefs. I was fascinated by the tales but also by the fact that here, hundreds of miles from civilization, a woman still had enough vanity to curl her hair each night.

"They've just had their first set of twins here in the village that they've let live," Mrs. Hawkins related. "Before we came with our own twins and persuaded them otherwise, the second twin born was considered a bad omen and was always killed." I shuddered at that. "You'll see the little ones tomorrow," she continued. "They're just adorable."

And so we did. Next morning the mother presented herself at the house, a round little brown baby on each hip, the slings for them crisscrossing between her breasts. They were identical...except for the red bead strung on a cord around the neck of the one that had been born first.

Don and I left Diana with Mrs. Hawkins and toured the village with her husband. The Indians, grinning their toothsome grins, were happy to show us their homes. Their somewhat Oriental facial features portrayed both intelligence and a sense of humor.

"I wish I could paint their portraits," I murmured to Don as we watched them completing a house, weaving the leaf roof. "Their faces are so appealing and they seem so happy all the time."

A group of women were making cassava bread which later we shared as we watched two men demonstrate a wrestling match, which was their way of settling disagreement. The community bowl we were offered to dunk our cassava bread in was enormous. It could have served as a baby bath.

We left later that day, taking with us numerous Wai Wai handicrafts and more numerous blessings, especially for the little white baby. The air was vibrant with prayers as Don ran up the engine. The men had, indeed, cleared another ten feet for the airstrip but Don still instructed them to hold the plane back as long as they could so he could get as much power as possible for the take-off. Mrs. Pryor, who was heavier than I, sat in the front seat holding Diana. In the back seat, I leaned my weight as far forward as possible. What with all the prayers outside the plane and Mrs. Pryor, her eyes squeezed shut in fervent prayer, I half expected to look out and see the Holy Father perched on a wing-tip.

Perhaps I missed Him. Our Tri-Pacer grazed the tops of the trees at the end of the airstrip as a communal sigh of relief filled the cabin. Don smiled and winked back at me as he banked and turned in the direction of Lumid Pau and his precious gas tanks.

18

The Man in Khaki

As the months stretched on in our lush green valley, my admiration for this man I was living with stretched also. I had known from the beginning that his middle name was "perseverance," but his dogged determination in spite of floods, delays, and stupid mistakes on the part of the crew, simply amazed me. He slept well at night, not only from exhaustion, but also because whatever he attempted, the motive was sound, his conscience untroubled. No moral gray areas there.

It had taken a year to the day after we stepped off the plane at Atkinson Field to get the mining equipment functioning. In that time Don was not only a would-be diamond miner and skillful pilot, but also had adopted the skills of: engineer, mechanic, electrician, plumber, carpenter, farmer, storekeeper, and a fair amount of doctoring. He had learned, and taught me, to say things like "more-cake-oh-mwa-horn-ah" (Hi!) to the Macusis and helped me form in Brazilian the most critical sentences for doing the laundry or watching the children.

Don was keenly aware that the mining equipment was precious—and irreplaceable. He had learned at the company we'd purchased it from as much about maintaining and repairing it as he could before we left the U.S. Once in British Guiana, he was strictly on his own and would have to figure out the rest by himself. His learning was by trial and error— *many* errors, but never the same one twice.

In addition to being my "teacher," he was my guide, my prompter, my friend, and, after he learned that laughing at my fears *really* got my goat, my ally. He was the positive to my negative, the joie de vivre to my angst, the idea man with head in the clouds (figuratively as well as literally) to my pragmatism. We worked well as a team.

As his soul mate, my heart ached for him when impatient investors back in Wisconsin took pot shots, suggesting he couldn't possibly be doing his best to get the mining operation going. Their impatience was understandable: when a machine part didn't fit in the 'States, they'd pick up the phone and order another. Such luxuries were not available to us. Don had to figure it out on his own. Barges had to be built for the equipment while riverbeds were being explored for optimum diamond-bearing gravel. This part they may have anticipated and endured. But what they couldn't have foreseen was a crew assembled and ready to go and a river that wouldn't cooperate. Or a compliant river perfect for starting up the dredging engines, but a crew's departure for a holiday celebration. Or, that Mario would be "billious" and couldn't work, and Pedro decided his earnings would allow him to go home to his wife for a fortnight.

"We've got the most billious crew in the whole damned world!" Don would say in disgust. "I sat on the barge by myself all day today, switching motors on and off and watching the men go up and down like a bunch of damned Jack-in-the-boxes! It takes them half an hour to put on their helmets and weights and then they pop back up because they've forgotten to ask me something." It hadn't been a good day.

Gasoline supplies for both the plane and the mining equipment had to be planned carefully. We kept a good supply at Marquis, of course, but Don wanted "stashes" of aviation gas strategically placed at various airstrips in the savannahs, so that he knew when he left on a flight in the morning, he'd be able to get back again if his flight plan changed. He would try to store his barrels of gas where nearby Indians could keep an eye on them for him. There were small plane pilots in the area who were not above helping themselves to our precious gas supply "in an emergency" ...or not.

I tried to keep the household running smoothly. There, at least, I had some element of control. So I called on Mario, Dutch, or whoever was in sight to keep our generator filled with gasoline or remove the snake found to be the reason the kitchen sink wasn't draining properly. (Don't you just hate it when a six foot boa clogs the drain?) Don had more important problems to solve.

At least he had his pride and joy as well as a diversion— the radio transmitter and receiver. If the generator was running we had communication with Georgetown. Two radio crystals, one set for B.G. Airways and the other for Cable and Wireless, allowed us to make calls, if not to receive them. If someone wanted to reach us, they'd have to arrange an "appointment" through Cable and Wireless, who would in turn notify us so that we could connect at the appointed time. Of course anyone else in the country with a radio transmitter was also trying to connect with Georgetown in those same hours, but with persistence—and if it was really urgent—Don could get through.

Don's store was the Neiman Marcus of the interior. An awesome assortment of cotton fabrics that only a man could select—we had no control over our agent in town in this regard— took front stage and center when the drop down door/counter was opened for business. Pink satins sat beside garish cotton prints. Cheap and full of sizing, after one washing in the river a dress sewn from these would be limp and lifeless. Pink panties were stacked beside paper fans that advised "Keep Cool and Be Gay." Hair goo was a must for the men. Kkaki pants and shirts, of course, were a necessity. Weeping bags of brown sugar sat next to equally large sacks of rice and flour and the smell of garlic and onions permeated it all. The customers loved that store.

It was behind the counter that Don became a linguist of sorts. His Macusi and Brazilian phrases were funny to the Indians and Brazilians. But we risked the embarrassment, because when the Indians tried out English, we were not so much chuckling as stymied.

One morning while we sat at our breakfast table next to the window, two Indians appeared on the other side of the screen.

"You got skorchip?" one asked earnestly. Don and I looked at each other, puzzled. "Skorchip?" we pronounced in unison.

"Skorchip! SKORCHIP!" the Indian repeated insistently.

Both Don and I still looked blank. With a complete exasperation, the Indian reached in his companion's pocket and pulled out his handkerchief.

"Skorchip! Skorchip" he cried, waving it at us.
These stupid white people need props!

At least that time there *were* props. I wasn't so lucky when later a Macusi family, after watching me through the screened windows for several minutes and deciding I wouldn't bite, ventured, "No guts turkey pots?"

I smiled, but the smile sat on a blank face. *Now what do I do?* I shrugged and held both hands out in supplication.

They all giggled. "No guts turkey pots?" They were having fun practicing their English, but I just stood there looking perplexed. We were getting nowhere.

Pointing toward the barracoun, I told them, "Go find Dutch," hoping he would be able to translate. But it bothered me the whole day. The "no guts" part was easy. "No got" was simpler than "Don't you have." But the "turkey pots" really had me stumped. Talking to myself I'd say it fast: "nogutsturkeypots." Nothing. I'd say it slowly: "No got turkey pots?" That seemed worse.

"Turkeypotsturkeypotsturkeypots!" A brilliant flash! *Storekeeper!* They were asking me if we had someone to sell them something down at the store.

As our bank account ran lower and lower, Don flew our plane more and more. Since the fatal crash of another bush pilot, Joe Tesarek, no one had been supplying the outposts along the Brazilian border. Don took that job over, flying in rations and store goods, often exchanging them for rough diamonds. When the rains came and travel by foot was nearly impossible, Don ferried not only cargo but passengers as well.

Income from the flying kept us and the mining company going. Once, after delivering an important Brazilian politician to a critical meeting, Don received a sort of *carte blanche* for flying over the Brazilian border and landing on nearby airstrips. General Valois decreed that, since Don had such a great reputation for helping everyone out, he was not to be bothered by any officials. Valois' signature at the bottom of our official "permit" was impressive.

Unfortunately Boa Vista was a little further inside the Brazilian border than Don's usual destinations and little men with big guns at the airstrip weren't impressed with any signature. They had their orders for foreign aircraft landing without prior permission.

In his first book, Don describes his encounter with the armed Brazilians from Boa Vista in great detail, and who am I to correct any of it? He and I have *discussed* the length of his absence countless times, all such discussion ending with his decree that "If *we* can't agree on how long I was under arrest, then who else is there to question it?" *My* side of the story—not nearly as exciting as his tales of sheets tied to the bed to enable his escape from "house arrest" in a filthy Brazilian hotel, or other tales of crawling on his belly three miles to the airstrip to fly off at daylight—borders on the mundane.

Don had dropped me and our two toddlers at Good Hope that Friday, saying he'd be back for tea after a quick flight to Lethem. Expecting we'd be back home that night, I'd brought just a couple of diapers and a jar of baby food. Silly me. That was the last I saw of Don for the next three days.

Thank God I was at Good Hope and that Caesar had flown with Don to Lethem. Had I been at Marquis, no telling how I would have gotten word of where my husband was. But Caesar was able to get back to Good Hope from Lethem by Jeep that night and told us of Don's mercy mission to Boa Vista.

"Padre Marco persuaded Don to take a very sick Brazilian girl over to Boa Vista for treatment," Caesar explained. "When Don hesitated at making the illegal flight, the Padre said he would even go along to speak for Don so that officials would okay his landing." Nellie and I sat at the dinner table listening to Caesar as he explained the events of the day.

"Doc Diamond wanted to go over to Brazil and check on the new rumor that hoof-and-mouth disease was breaking out again over there, so he went along, too. We all thought it

Don and Harry in our trade store

would be okay and that Don, Doc, and the Padre would be right back. Obviously it wasn't."

Well, at least I knew he was alive. But Saturday was a long day of waiting without word. On Sunday night when Don finally managed to get a radio message through to Normandy, an outpost just across the river from Good Hope, we learned a little bit more. He was under house arrest, his *carte blanche* doing him no good since General Valois and accompanying officials were all off celebrating Carnival in Manaus and couldn't be reached. Doc and Padre Marco were free to go, but were hanging around trying to secure Don's and the plane's release.

That information relieved us somewhat. I would have been a whole lot happier with the appearance of a dozen diapers, clean clothes for the three of us, and a few small jars of baby food. Fortunately we could mash bananas for baby Tom.

When General Valois' telegram reached Boa Vista on Monday with instructions to let Don go, the men with guns did so grudgingly. Back at Good Hope, Don found me out in the bathroom washing diapers for the fifth or sixth time, Diana running around naked, and Tom looking glum in nothing but a slightly damp diaper. By that time, I'd donned some clothes Pixie had left behind in her closet. Of course Don had neither shaved nor showered, let alone changed clothes, for three days. "We make a fine family portrait," I laughed, throwing my irritation aside for once. Relief and reunion were powerful antidotes to my pique.

Before finally deciding on a BS degree in Economics, Don had contemplated medicine as a profession and spent three years in Pre-Med at UW in Madison. Just as our plane became more and more important to inhabitants of the interior, so did Don's ability to "doctor" in times of need. In fact, when Dr. Talbot in Lethem got wind of Don's medical "talents" he enlisted his aid numerous times, even as anesthetist for an emergency appendectomy.

"Boy, I didn't like doing that!" Don exclaimed when he got back from Lethem that night. "Reminded me of when I was little and they gave me ether to set my broken arm. I had all I could do today to keep from throwing up! But the patient survived, thank God."

Fortunately our little family stayed healthy from beginning to end of our stay in South America. Bites from the cabourri fly sometimes became infected and required penicillin ointment. But we had a healthy supply of Caladryl in our medicine chest and used it to head off the scratching that inevitably opened the bites. Don's feet were vulnerable to fungal invasions since he worked in or near the river and shoes were a must. Several nights found him reading by kerosene lamp while soaking his feet in hot water laced with potassium permanganate. Picture this: a husband with purple feet and ankles and children white-spotted with Caladryl.

With the help of doctor friends in the 'States, we'd put together a complete medicine chest before we left for South America. And of course we had *Merck's Medical Manual* within reach at all times. Not that we needed to worry about running out of penicillin! It had reached the interior with the reputation of a cure-all. Brazilians and Indians alike used it topically and internally for any and all ailments. Some even took penicillin shots daily as a preventative, much as we take vitamins. They wondered why Don didn't carry hypodermic needles in his shop!

The two plagues of the Rupununi boiled down to biliousness and skin infections. Feeling bilious was, in fact, to be constipated, and if one considers the diet of farine and salt-dried beef, this is not surprising. Now how could we have forgotten Ex-Lax when packing our medicine box?

But the natives had faith in medicine and they had faith in Don. With his box of magic powders Don, then, was infallible in their eyes. And so Rosina thought when she brought her little daughter to us one day.

"Sumtin wrong," she said, pointing at the child's legs wrapped in filthy cotton rags. Don carefully unwrapped them to reveal huge open sores covering both legs. I gasped and even Don was taken aback at the sight of them. Mother and child were stoic.

"No more cabourri bites," he cautioned Rosina after washing, drying, and applying medicated powder to the sores. "You must keep her legs covered until they heal," he instructed and Rosina nodded her compliance.

"Here, take these, Rosina," I said, handing her a pair of Diney's pink cotton overalls. It would be protection from bites as well as helping to keep the child's legs clean. "Let us know how she does."

A few weeks later, I spotted Rosina on the compound and asked how her little girl's legs were doing.

"I treat dem wit juice from tree and dey much betta," she smiled. "But bes ting is small pants you give. Dey make Vwanda all good again."

Of course the natives lived in that medical limbo between age-old remedies passed down through generations and the modern day medicine of the "civilized" world. And, just as we took our knowledge to them, they in turn advised us of their firm beliefs.

When I was pregnant with Diana, Don and I flew with the Gorinskys to visit an old Brazilian woman and her husband on the other side of the Ireng River. As we women sat chatting, I drew my legs up to sit cross-legged on the floor—a most comfortable position for me since it afforded a space for my belly to hang. The old woman moved quickly to my side saying quietly that I must never, never sit that way. Her look was serious.

Nellie, seeing my consternation, explained the woman's belief that if I sat cross-legged, my child would be cross-legged inside of me and never be able to get out.

Now that I could handle. But when later I learned a Brazilian midwife had hung Pedro Bandido's wife up by her heels on the discovery the baby was a breech, I was incredulous of such ignorance. Though Francesca miraculously survived, the baby was born dead.

"There is so much for them to learn," I said to Don on one occasion. "So much for us to teach them. Ignorance is a terrible thing."

"I agree," Don replied. "Just today I met up with Dutch on the path, and he was muttering and shaking his head as only Dutch can do. He'd just found Toman Davis' wife putting glue on her child's face."

"Glue!" I cried. "What on earth…?"

"Well, the tube she found in some trash pile was such a lovely shade of light green, and since it had a red and yellow label on it she figured it had to be an okay cream for her baby's face," he explained, a wry smile on his face.

"Oh, no," I groaned. "The poor child…"

Doctoring often got in the way of piloting and mining and sometimes we couldn't tell the difference between real emergency and sly conniving. Such as the day Chaga's pregnant wife, Maria, came down to Marquis from the mine site up-river, complaining of pains even though, she said, her time wasn't near.

"Can we take the chance?" Don asked me. He was loath to drag himself away from pressing matters to fly Maria out. "What if it's something serious? I'd never forgive myself."

"Go then. Just be quick about it," I urged, casting a worried eye at poor Maria, whose pains seemed to be increasing as she sat in our living room. So he dropped what he was doing and flew Maria and the rest of her family and belongings to the nearest midwife, twenty miles away.

Two months later, Maria, even greater with child, found her way back up to Marquis and came to me in the house.

"Yes, Mistress," she smiled through her dark and broken teeth. "I guess I still gots a leetle while to go." Bag, baggage, and other children in tow, she headed back up-river to the mine site to wait for "her time."

"Was it a fight with her husband a couple months ago?" I said to Don that night. "Or was she homesick? Or do you think she really had a medical problem?"

"We'll never know, will we?" Don smiled, his conscience clear.

19

Flying Ants

We greeted our third rainy season with mixed feelings. The bounty from our garden would be welcomed for the variety it gave to our menus. I dreaded the fight against mold growing on our shoes in the closet and the mildew on the walls.

When I took Diana home to meet her grandparents in '56, I missed most of the rainy season but heard Don's wonderful tales of fishing at Karanambo in the Crane Pond.

"You should've seen them! Don enthused when we were next together. "Hundreds of them flying in to build their nests in the trees around the pond. First there'd be a cloud of pink and then a cloud of white. I've never seen anything like it!"

Karanambo, like many of the homesteads dotting the savannah, became an island in rainy season. Instead of meeting the mail plane every two weeks by jeep, the McTurks would travel by boat from house to airstrip.

In September of '57 when we returned to Marquis with baby Tommy, the rains had ceased, the melons were gone, tomatoes on their way out, and the corn well past the stamina of human teeth and jaws. Dutch had consumed as many melons as was humanly possible and given the rest away to the crew, though they didn't appreciate them the way we did. But with no teeth, Dutch could only enjoy even the earliest, tender ears of corn.

But we were all in residence for the four soggy months of rainy season '58. Right on cue, it rained on April first and from that date a clothesline zigzagged its way across the guestroom, so that diapers and clothes could dry. Or so we wished. They hung there for days on end but still felt damp. It was hard to tell which diapers I'd just taken off Tommy and which were about to go on him. *Ah, yes, this one emits a faint odor of ammonia. Put the other one on..*

Fortunately, we got a week of really dry weather in July and scurried about airing clothes, shoes, hammocks, and linens on lines strung outside in the sun. But the downpour resumed, and we all shouted to be heard above the drumbeat of it on our corrugated tin roof. Marquis was flooded from the airstrip to the step-down bathroom in the house. And with the rain came the bugs.

Fortunately the house was screened. But those screens were plugged with heavily oiled cabourri flies. The breezes died in rainy season so there was nothing to move the heavy, moisture-filled air along. No wonder the clothes hanging inside and on our bodies couldn't dry. The cabourris outside were mini vampires. Though it was hot and humid, to venture outside meant dressing in long pants, long sleeved shirts, socks and shoes, and a scarf covering all but my eyes.

"The tomato garden is beginning to look like the Hollywood backdrop for a Tarzan movie," I reported to Don one morning. "Cabourris or no, I'm going out to prune them back. We'll find them vining into the kitchen pretty soon!" Dressed as if for the frigid north, out I went.

Huge flying ants, meanwhile, were holding a mating festival inside the house. These crawled in every crack and crevice of the house in one night and invaded our

Tommy

belongings. In the following months we'd be shaking them out of towels from the linen closet, unopened Kleenex boxes, and between the sheets of our beds. Diana the Brave would wield a mean flyswatter that third summer, while I swept mounds of dead ants out the back door.

Of course moths were attracted to the kerosene lamps we burned at night, or to the electric lights we occasionally turned on when the generator was running. Droves of fluttering insects took up residence and formed their cocoons everywhere, including inside our pillowcases. Diana had quite a cocoon collection in jars, fascinated as only a three-year-old can be with how a "worm" can turn into a "butterfye." No "moffs" for her. Each morning she'd climb down from her crib, run to her collection, pick out the best specimen, and bring it to us in bed. There is just no substitute for waking to the nervous flutter of a huge, hairy moth on one's pillow.

But if the flying creatures were unwelcome, the frogs with their little sucker feet were almost my undoing. I dreaded cleaning the bathroom— their favorite haunt. I knew no matter how watchful I was, a nasty little frog would leap out from behind a hanging towel or a cake of soap in the shower and land wherever his little clinging feet could find bare skin. I hated them!

"Jan, let's take a little break, just the two of us, and fly over to Caracas for a week," Don suggested one evening in the middle of the summer. "It would be our first real break in two years and I know Nellie would be more than delighted to have the kids at Good Hope, while we're gone." He didn't have to wait for my answer. I had started planning my travel wardrobe after the first few words.

The two of us packed what finery we could gather, dropped Diana and Tommy at Nellie and Caesar's, and flew into Georgetown, gleeful as a couple of kids. The Woodbine

Hotel was full, so we checked into the Tower Hotel and raced to leave our passports at the American Consulate to get our visas for Venezuela in order. Pam Wheating had planned a gala cocktail party for the night before we were to fly off, and we didn't want to miss it.

"Well *that* was a proper send-off!" Don grinned when we got back to the Tower that night. Exhausted from the day's errands and the evening's merriment, we fell into bed and slept soundly.

Next morning, I got no further than the dressing table before realizing we had been burgled. My jewelry, wallet, money, glasses with gold wire on the frame, Don's glasses, sunglasses, money, and manicure set—all gone. Fortunately, our passports were still at the American Consulate ready to be picked up on our way to the airport. More fortunately, we had thrown our dirty laundry on top of $4000 worth of rough diamonds in the corner of the bathroom behind the toilet. We'd arrived in Georgetown too late to take the parcel to the bank and we were savvy enough to know no one gives anything of value to the front desk for safe-keeping. The laundry pile was our best bet and it succeeded.

Of course our trip to Venezuela was off. We spent the day waiting for police to appear and watching them painstakingly write down our account of the robbery. Nothing was ever printed in the newspaper. The hotel manager's father owned controlling interest in all three Georgetown papers, so any adverse publicity concerning the hotel was hushed up.

"I'm so disgusted with the way this thing is being handled by the police," Don snapped. Let's do a little detective work on our own. Maybe it'll help us work off some of our wrath!" It did. And it gave us an immense sense of satisfaction that we learned more about *what* occurred *when*, than the officials did.

Not that it helped to catch the thief or thieves. I left careful drawings of each piece of jewelry, so the police could pass them out to the city pawnbrokers. It took them seven weeks, we later learned, to distribute these. By the end of our "week's vacation," discouraged and just wanting to put the whole incident behind us, we decided to fly back to the Rupununi, gather up our children, and go home for the rest of the dreary rainy season.

"Just being back at Marquis makes me grateful and just look at all these bounties the season provides," I ventured, trying to think positively. "Our drinking water never gets dangerously low, and we can practically watch the garden grow." *Along with the mildew on the walls, I thought, grabbing my bottle of Clorox.*

Dutch had planted corn in early May, and by the end of June we were eating the first tender ears slathered in butter and salt. It was cattle corn to be sure, but if picked at just the right moment before it was entirely ripe, it was delicious.

We brought in watermelons by the half dozen, so the refrigerator sagged with their weight. We took some as gifts to neighbors as we flew about the savannahs. Tomatoes and muskmelons hung heavy on their vines and our papaya trees yielded brilliant orange fruits by the dozens. Don would hoist little Diney up to where they hung, and she would toss them down to me. What fun!

In August, as the rains subsided , papaya slices with a wedge of lime graced our dining table for breakfast, lunch, and dinner. We never tired of the mangoes Don brought back from his flying trips. We considered them one of God's finest creations and never had too many.

Don's flying took him to an airstrip called Velgrad, so named by a settler whose home it had been in Yugoslavia. Don bought rough diamonds here from Matt Tesarek, brother of another bush pilot, Joe Tesarek. At Velgrad a

Picking papayas

"forest" of avocado trees bore fruit as if to corner the world market. With an overburden of avocados there, Don started trading in them, delivering bags of "green gold" by plane to his other airstrips. Or, spreading them out on the floor of our guestroom, awaiting distribution to other outposts.

"It's a darned good thing we're not expecting any guests!" I laughed one day in the middle of all this. "What with clotheslines festooned with damp diapers and a floor covered with ripening avocados, our "guestroom" is anything but!"

The tidy untidiness of that room and the scene outside my kitchen window in the rainy seasons at Marquis, *more* than compensated for the moldy shoes. As did hundreds of morning glory vines twining in and out of the cornfields, papaya trees, and scrub brush between our house and the river. Dry season could never have painted such beauty and color. Added to this, money was there to be made as Don's business of supplying rations and transporting people throughout the flooded savannah nearly tripled in that rainy season. So it was with a certain sense of well-being that we fell asleep to the deafening sound of torrential rains falling on the corrugated tin roof. At least it didn't leak and we were snug and dry—relatively—in our beds. That summer we read all the Agatha Christie mysteries in print. The pouring rain and darkness created an ideal mood and background.

But as mid-August approached, rainy season tapered off and occasionally we'd have a night so clear and bright with stars we just had to get outside to enjoy it.

"No cabourris after dark, you know," Don said after dinner on one such night. "After we get the kids in bed, let's you and me take the cot and the map outside and look at the constellations."

I readily agreed in spite of the fact that he was referring to our canvas army cot, too narrow for one, much less two of us. With no television and the radio producing only a disembodied voice listing the events of a world way beyond our reach, stargazing and constellation-finding was our evening's entertainment. We'd ordered a Map of the Heavens from National Geographic months before, and had even seen the Russian satellite, Sputnik, cross the sky from one range of "our mountains" to the other. Moving slowly, it flashed off and on, off and on. And we were mesmerized.

Next day we were back in reality. That's when Ramdat came down with chicken pox and the cesspit collapsed. It had been Dutch's construction, his talent for underground creations being about the same as those he used for building our hangar on Marquis airstrip.

"I'll fix the pit before we fly Ramdat into town," Don offered. And I was more than grateful for *that* order of things.

"I go help Daddy," announced Diney, excited by this new turmoil in the house.

"Better you than I!" I replied, already forcing myself to conjure the scents of roses, frangipani, and gardenias for my olfactory senses. That was the day Diney learned her first cuss words helping Daddy.

Fortunately, repairing the cesspit didn't take long and we took off with Ramdat for Georgetown. "The kids haven't had their vaccinations for chicken pox yet, and Ramdat's been carrying Tommy around for the last week. Come to think of it, they haven't had smallpox vaccinations yet either," I said over the run-up sound of the engine. "You don't think it's smallpox do you?" I asked, suddenly filled with dread.

"Worry won't help," Don replied. We'll soon know what we're dealing with." And off we flew, just ahead of the black clouds of another downpour, Ramdat in the backseat looking like his own seven days' rain.

We hoped for a quick diagnosis and quick recovery for him, knowing that life would be better when Ramdat returned to his post. But Ramdat never did.

20

The Grand Finale

On those nights during the rainy season of '58 when the rains would abate and we *could* hear each other, Don and I talked about winding down our life in South America.

"It's not that we haven't tried, Hon," I said, not for the first time that summer. "We've had no help from the investors this year, but with all your flying and trading, we're in better financial shape than we've ever been. We don't have any more outstanding bills and even have some money of our own put aside."

"We also don't have much of a mining operation left," Don replied ruefully. "Sometimes I think we've got more equipment on the bottom of the Ireng River than on the barges." The silence of the night, punctuated only by the song of the tree frogs, was the stage for resignation, not depression. "Let's face it, we won't have either money or new equipment coming from the 'States, not to mention any encouragement."

"Well, we can't blame the investors either. I think their dream was bigger and even more unrealistic than ours," I sighed.

Meanwhile, Don kept flying almost constantly, weather

conditions permitting. He was supplying outposts, buying diamonds from the "pork knockers" there and making a concerted effort to collect old debts. For one he was given payment in the form of a good bull, which prompted a side business of cattle trading. Keeping the cattle at Marquis was not a problem. We had plenty of grazing land beside the airstrip and soon had acquired enough cattle to constitute a shipment of beef to Georgetown.

"I'll get Toman Davis to drive them to Good Hope and then to the abattoir at Lethem," Don announced one morning at the end of rainy season. "He ought to be able to get two or three willing Indians to help him. We've got twenty head and that's plenty for a shipment of beef to Georgetown. Gosh, Jan, I'm actually seeing some progress here!" he said happily.

In fact, those last four months in British Guiana were the happiest of all for us. Having made the decision to rely solely on ourselves for income and payments of company debts, we felt free to pursue whatever it was we could do to wind up our "adventurous life." I flew more and more with Don, knowing Diana and Tommy were safe with Noreen, whom they adored. I'd called this country "home" for over three years and having come to terms with it now wanted to take a last look at it from a more nostalgic point of view.

"Hey, Jan," Don exclaimed as he strode in the front door on return from a flight to Good Hope. "We've been invited to a party for one of the Melville clan who's leaving the Rupununi for England. It's next Saturday in Lethem and we can take the kids and stay overnight in Teddy Melville's hotel there. This sounds like fun!"

Indeed it did. Rupununi parties were legendary, sometimes resembling a three-ring circus and always lasting more than just an evening. "I hope you accepted the invitation!" I replied and got a vigorous nod and a wink in return.

Don had a heavy flying schedule for that Saturday but insisted he could fit it all in and still get us to Lethem in time for the party. I had us all packed and ready to take off by late afternoon, but the sun was ominously low on the horizon when I finally heard the hum of our Cessna's engine.

Diney and I ran to the airstrip as Don turned the plane back to get ready for an immediate take-off. Noreen carried Tommy. Bent over and hobbling as usual, Dutch scurried behind her carrying his meager parcel of his clothes and his false teeth—*this* was an occasion. They reached the plane just as I opened the door. There was not a minute to lose. Darkness comes on quickly in the tropics and we had a twenty-five minute flight ahead of us. It was a breathtaking flight in the sunset but we were grateful to get out of the hills and valleys to the flat savannah by the time it got dark.

Finding Lethem was not a problem. It would be a cluster of lights in the enveloping darkness ten minutes further on. But finding the airstrip, even though it was large enough to accommodate a DC-3, would be a little trickier.

"I'll fly over Teddy's hotel to get a fix on the airstrip," Don began… just as the runway was bathed in a sea of light. We looked at each other and grinned. "Someone, probably Caesar, knew we'd be calling it close. He must have rounded up every vehicle with working headlights in town and lined them up on either side of the strip. Good for him…and us!" Actually it was the District Commissioner, Eric Coussou, who organized it all. At the sound of our plane's engine, he'd given the signal for them all to switch on their lights. If Caesar hadn't been already having a whale of a time at the party, I'm sure he would have been on hand to read us the riot act.

It was a party all right! *That* was the night made famous by the dog that ran off with Dutch's teeth. We danced, we sang and the rum flowed. It was good to laugh again. Diana and Tommy, snug in their beds on the floor above missed it all. But they felt livelier in the morning than we did.

There were several celebrations at Marquis too that summer. We flew the McTurks in to help us celebrate our anniversary with champagne and the first leg of lamb we'd had in over a year. When Don flew them home next day, he picked up Nellie, Caesar and their new baby, Marc, to help us celebrate Tommy's first birthday.

The afternoon became somewhat of a circus when a small plane carrying two Americans flew in and landed at our airstrip. They'd come for advice from Don so he sat and tried to talk seriously with them about doing business in B.G.—all to the accompaniment of birthday celebrations in the background. To complete the chaotic cartoon, Don was soaking one foot in a pan of scalding water, purple with potassium permanganate, in an effort to dislodge a nasty infection. Hammocks hung from every available beam and hook that night.

With the end of the year drawing closer, Don and I wrote to ask our parents to come down for a visit before we pulled up stakes. "You'll never be able to duplicate a trip like this," we wrote both his parents and mine. Of course we got nowhere with my parents, but we kept coaxing Eleanor and Erv Haack in every weekly letter.

"Well, there's good news and there's bad news," Don announced on his return from a Friday mail run to Good Hope. "It's not really *bad* news, but it sure makes me mad. He handed me a letter from the police at the Lethem station.

I took it all in with a glance. "I guess we know whose work this is," I said wryly. "Who else but Valerie is spiteful enough to start a petition to stop us from 'flying for reward' in the interior? Never mind that we're also trying to help people." The letter directed Don that henceforth, should he fly either cargo or passengers for payment, the authorities would seize our plane.

"'Not to worry,' as Nellie says," Don continued. Here's the good news: Mom and Dad finally decided to take us up on our invitation to visit before we leave B.G. Of course, we won't be able to charge them for the flight," he finished with a grin. "They should be here late in September."

Which they were, arriving in Georgetown the day *before* we heard of it on our receiver via B.G Airways radio. "Jan! Mother and Dad are in Georgetown!" Don called from his radio room. "They've been there since yesterday and wonder why we weren't there to meet them!"

"Meet me at the airstrip," he called over his shoulder as he dashed out the door. A startled Noreen took Tommy from my arms as I rushed off to grab our toothbrushes and a change of clothes.

"We'll be back tomorrow with Don's parents," I said to Noreen who was, as usual, as calm as ever, taking this new development in stride. I could sense that she was already planning the next day's dinner for all of us. What a blessing she was!

From the minute Eleanor and Erv arrived in the Rupununi, they were thrilled with everything: Diana and Tommy, of course, Bambi, flights with Don to far-flung outposts, the Indians and Brazilians, Caesar and Nellie and the other ranchers in the savannah. Besides the fishing at Karanambo, they were treated to a jeep ride by Tiny McTurk. They hadn't gone far from the house before a baby cayman ran out in front of the jeep. In a flash, Tiny and Don were out of the vehicle and after the cayman. Tiny caught him by the tail and brought him back for Erv and Eleanor's up close inspection. I thought they would expire from sheer delight.

Even the cabourri flies couldn't discourage them. They attacked Eleanor's ankles with a vengeance. "Don't worry, Jan," she said as I surveyed her swollen feet and legs. "They seem to be worst in the late afternoon, so I'll just stay inside, prop my feet up and do some mending. She did more repair of the buttonless and ripped in three weeks than I'd done in three years!

But the day came when the doting grandparents had to be pulled away from adoring grandchildren and flown to Georgetown for their return to civilization. Leaving Diney and Tom with Noreen, once again—all three of them crying—Don and I, Eleanor and Erv took off from Marquis and headed north. For one last thrill, Don flew the four of us over Kaiteur Falls—*over* being the operative word! Flying as low over the river as was prudent, we approached the falls, suddenly everything below the plane dropped away. Then Don side slipped the plane beside the falling water and into the spray beyond the falls. The communal gasp from at least three of us was audible above the noise of the plane's engine.

Don and I agreed that his parents' visit couldn't have been more perfect. "I know your mother is glad to see the end of the cabourri flies, though," I remarked after we'd seen them off in the taxi to Atkinson. "Her ankles were beginning to look like raw hamburger meat!"

Back home at Marquis, the kids loved the excitement provided by packing up one life and getting ready for another. Boxes piled in the living room were marked for the Red Cross in Georgetown, Nellie at Good Hope, and missionaries scattered throughout the Rupununi. There was not much in the way of clothing to be taken back to the 'States. After three years' pounding on the rocks of the Ireng River, our clothes were threadbare. In fact, we had dressmakers working overtime in Georgetown to get Diney and me presentable once we landed, in wintertime, in the 'States. My mother took on the task of buying winter coats for me and the children, then shipped them down to arrive in Georgetown before we did. Don knew he could always wrap himself in a blanket provided by a kindly stewardess.

My excitement at returning to the 'States was catching. "I think you're trying to brainwash them," Don joked as I showed the children their new shoes and a bright red patent leather purse for Diney. Having been barefooted most of their young lives, neither got very excited about the shoes. But Diney ran to find nickles and dimes to put in her new purse "for buy icekweem in 'States."

Packing was becoming an almost insurmountable problem. Monstrous items like a crib and a playpen presented a packaging challenge when all we had in the house and on the compound were odd boxes from the trade store and bits and pieces of string on hand. Fifteen-month-old Tommy tore into the cartons of toys destined for the missionaries and delighted in death defying jumps from boxes he could climb on. Where would we have been without Noreen?

"Dinner is ready, Miss Jan," she'd announce as she threaded her way to the dining room table through misplaced furniture and boxes both full and empty. She hid her sadness at the thought of our departure. She had been a godsend to us and in a way, we to her. This had been the adventure of her life, living in the beautiful interior of her country, reading Dr. Seuss to her two charges, and making life easier for two foreigners. She was a remarkable woman to have adapted so well.

"I think I've got a solid buyer for the plane!" Don announced one day at the beginning of our last week at Marquis. "The new police director at MacKenzie was interested but never offered to put down a deposit. (MacKenzie was an American bauxite mine south of Georgetown and had it's own airstrip.) "But now that insurance guy, Henry Fitt, says he wants it and has offered earnest money as a deposit.

"That's a load off our minds! I replied happily. Henry Fitt was also my hairdresser's husband, so I recognized the name. Little did I know then that I might royally screw up *that* transaction within a week.

Considering the finality of the curtain being dropped on this segment of our lives, we had to make sure we said proper goodbyes to those who had figured so prominently in this never-to-be-forgotten adventure. We did the best we could to make sure no one would be overlooked or wished well. But the day came when we had to close the door to our house and start down the path to the airstrip one last time. Noreen would come along to Georgetown with us, holding baby Tommy as closely as possible for as long as possible. But Dutch was a thin, bent and forlorn figure next to the runway as the plane roared past him on take-off. The battered old hat came off in salute causing an enormous lump to fill my throat.

With only two days before our flight left for New York, our work in Georgetown was cut out for us. But I managed to make an appointment with my hairdresser right away and left the children with Noreen who was happy to have them to herself one last time.

As the hot water washed the dust of the Rupununi out of my hair and down the drain, I began to enjoy my hour of relaxation. "I'll bet you're pleased with your new plane," I offered by way of conversation to Mrs. Fitt as she wrapped the towel tightly around my wet head.

The expression on her face made me desperate to inhale the words back. In the half minute of silence that followed, I realized her husband had not told her of this transaction with Don. I hoped then that I'd faint and not have to finish what I'd started. But I didn't and waited when she excused herself for a few minutes while I was left to contemplate how I'd relate this all to Don.

My hair dried and done, mostly in awkward silence, I rushed back to the hotel, hoping my quick confession to Don would help save the day. It didn't. During the few minutes she'd left me alone she had made a phone call…to the bank requesting a stop payment on any large checks made out by her husband. I expected Don to be furious with me, but he didn't have time for that luxury. He was off like a shot to undo the mess I had caused.

Don and Henry Fitt closeted themselves somewhere unbeknownst to their wives. For hours. Don wanted to sell the plane. Henry wanted to buy it. I wanted him to buy it too. The price had been agreed upon and a down payment had been made. All systems had been go. But the power of one woman should never be underestimated.

My nerves were frazzled by the time Don strode through the door to the hotel dining room as I helped the children with their dinner. He wore a smile and held up a cashier's check. "The plane is sold. Let's eat."

How did Henry Fitt ever get his wife to agree to the purchase of our plane? We've pondered that one for years.

Next morning, as the taxi headed for Atkinson Field, Don and I gazed out the windows at the huge Flamboyant trees lining the broad avenue that was Main Street. "I know what you're thinking," Don said and indeed, he did. We were both thinking of our last meal in the Rupununi, two days before.

As I cleaned my plate, Nellie watched with a smile. "Well, that's that," she said with a satisfied tone and a wink at Caesar. Don and I asked in one voice, "That's what?"

"Oh, just a little saying we Wapishana's have: 'If a stranger drinks creek water and eats laba (a type of wild deer), he will always return to our country.' I knew you'd drunk plenty of creek water in the past few years, but I just wasn't sure you'd eaten laba. Well, now you have," she finished, a broad triumphant smile on her handsome face as she touched the platter in front of her. It was this wise woman's little trick. And it worked.

Ladies and gentlemen, your attention please:
KLM Royal Dutch Airlines announces the
Departure of Flight 498 leaving Georgetown
for Curacao with connections for San Juan
and New York City.
All aboard please.

Epilogue

We went down to South America as two. We came back as four. For some it would have been adventure enough. But not for us. We made Connecticut our home for a year, Wisconsin for five more. By then we numbered six, adding Todd and Julie to our family of explorers. And by 1965 we found ourselves back beneath the palms.